P9-BTN-446

BURIED BENEATH
THE
BAOBAB TREE

BURIED BENEATH THE BAOBAB TREE

ADAOBI TRICIA NWAUBANI
WITH AFTERWORD BY VIVIANA MAZZA

KATHERINE TEGEN BOOKS
An Imprint of HarperCollins Publishers

To the girls and women of Nigeria,
in the hope that they may know brighter times than these

Katherine Tegen Books is an imprint of HarperCollins Publishers.

Buried Beneath the Baobab Tree
Text copyright © 2018 by Adaobi Tricia Nwaubani
Afterword copyright © 2018 by Viviana Mazza
All rights reserved. Printed in the United States of America.
No part of this book may be used or reproduced in any manner whatsoever without
written permission except in the case of brief quotations embodied in critical articles
and reviews. For information address HarperCollins Children's Books, a division of
HarperCollins Publishers, 195 Broadway, New York, NY 10007.
www.epicreads.com

Library of Congress Control Number: 2018933386

ISBN 978-0-06-269672-4

Typography by Joel Tippie
18 19 20 21 22   PC/LSCH   10 9 8 7 6 5 4 3 2 1
❖
First Edition

Fitchburg Public Library
5530 Lacy Road
Fitchburg, WI 53711

. . . They wrote the story on a column,
And on the great church-window painted
The same, to make the world acquainted
How their children were stolen away,
And there it stands to this very day . . .

—Robert Browning, "The Pied Piper of Hamelin"

BIG DREAMS

MY SWEETEST DREAMS UNFOLD when my eyes are wide open, after I roll my sleeping mat and begin my morning chores.

As I walk to the well from which every family in our section of the village fetches water, I dream of a new pair of shoes for church on Sunday, shimmering red and shining new like that of the golden-haired girl I saw singing on TV, instead of black and slack like the ones I've had since two Christmases ago.

As I bend my back to blow the wood beneath Mama's pot until the embers crackle with dancing flames, I dream of a more bounteous harvest, for Papa to reap more than enough corn and groundnuts and beans from his farms this year, so that we can eat our fill and have enough left over to sell for school fees.

As I thrust my hand into every cranny of the living room, veranda, corridor, and backyard with my broom, I dream of acing the Borno State scholarship exam and leaving home to attend the special boarding school for girls in Maiduguri, of being the first child in my entire family—nuclear and extended—who proceeds to university after secondary school instead of back to Papa's farm or straight to my husband's house.

As I open my mouth to say "good morning" to Mama and hand her the pan of sleeping oil with which to fry the *kosai* for Papa and my brothers to eat when they awake, I dream of standing in front of a classroom full of children and telling them, "A is for apple!"

As I tighten my fingers around my youngest brother, Jacob, and stand his naked body in the basin of lukewarm water, then smear him with soap, I dream of being a good wife who kneels to serve her husband his meals and who bears him healthy sons.

As I load my arms with the empty plates my brothers have left behind on their way out, some to the farm and some to school, I dream of a sister instead of only five brothers, another girl to help with all the chores.

As I dip my palm into the—

"Hurry up! Let's not be late. I don't want to stay back after school to wash the toilet!"

The voice of my best friend, Sarah, slams my dreaming shut. She is at the door, textbooks and notebooks in hand.

Like me, she is the one who does the morning chores. Her two sisters have left home, married to men in the village next to ours.

"Please, give me a minute," I say. "Let me just rub some Vaseline on my hands."

That is the good thing about dreaming with my eyes wide open. It's like molding a calabash from wet clay. Some other time, some other day, I can always continue from wherever I stop, or even start from the beginning all over again.

SOMETIMES AND ALWAYS

Singing familiar tunes or learning the lyrics to new ones. Telling ancient riddles and jokes. Whispering secrets that no other ears will hear. Guessing for how long the hills layered majestically high with dense rocks have lived, and the baobab trees with bulbous trunks and buttress roots that make them stand out like aliens in the sprawling savanna landscape.

Always hand in hand.

My best friend and I prancing side by side on our way to school.

KOBOKO

Malam Zwindila scratches the date into the right-hand corner of the blackboard with a tiny piece of chalk. Mistakenly, he writes Monday instead of Tuesday.

With a handful of fresh green leaves from the pile on the teacher's desk, he wipes the wrong date off and writes the correct one. Then he turns to the right-hand side of the classroom, where the boys sit.

"You! What is democracy?" he asks.

Danladi, son of the village head hunter, rises to his feet.

"Sir, democracy is . . . democracy is . . ."

Mr. Zwindila's eyes point elsewhere.

"You! What is democracy?"

Peter, whose three brothers are crippled from polio, gets to his feet.

"Sir, democracy is . . . errrr . . . it is when . . ."

"You! What is democracy?"

Ibrahim, a wizard who can calculate twenty-three times seventy-three without pen or calculator but who doesn't know the difference between *their* and *there*, stands to his feet.

"Sir, democracy is the government of all types of people."

Malam Zwindila tosses the pile of used leaves onto the teacher's desk and grabs his *koboko*.

"Some of you have brains made of sawdust," he says.

He runs his other hand from one end of the long, hard whip to the other, slowly. His eyes survey the class.

Those three boys have just earned ten strokes of the koboko each, either on their buttocks or their palms, depending on Malam Zwindila's mood.

Who is next?

It is difficult to believe that this man inflicting terror is the same man who stood on the altar in Christ the King Church nine months ago, watery-eyed as his lithe bride walked up the aisle.

But I am not afraid.

I remember everything Malam Zwindila taught us in the last class and the one before that and in every other one before.

He turns toward the girls' side.

He is about to point his eyes at Sarah when I stretch my hand high up in the air.

"Sir?"

"Yes?"

Back at home, Papa and my brothers sit in the living room and talk about the news on the radio while Mama and I sit in the corridor, or in the kitchen.

Back at home, Mama must keep quiet whenever Papa speaks, and I must never question anything he says.

Back at home, the men and boys know everything, but here in school, I know more than all the boys. Salt may laugh at shea butter when the sun shines, but when the rain falls, it must hide its head.

"Sir, democracy is the government of the people, for the people, and for . . . and by the people," I say.

Malam Zwindila keeps his eyes on me. He doesn't waver, he doesn't flutter, he doesn't utter a word.

He slams his koboko whip down on the teacher's table, hard and quick.

My heart jumps.

"Clap for her!" he yells.

The whole class claps, keeps clapping, and continues clapping.

PINEAPPLES AND LIMES

I GAZE LONGINGLY AT the two straps outlined underneath my best friend's white blouse. When will it be my turn to wear a bra?

She has pineapples; I have limes.

If only breasts were like tomatoes and onions, which were certain to grow succulent and healthy if you put them in good ground at the right time of the year, then watered and weeded weekly. So far, all my daily yanking in the bathroom has yielded no results.

"Just a year or two more," Mama says. "My breasts also took longer to come out. But look at me today."

TREE OF LIFE

SARAH AND I MUST get home from school as quickly as possible to begin our chores and homework, but the pendulous fruits of the baobab tree at the church junction seem to be calling our names.

We stop to answer, laying down our books beneath its cool shade. The temptation is too hard for us to resist.

Of all the tales Papa has told us when we've gathered around him under the light of the full moon, my favorite is about the baobab tree.

"A long, long time ago," he said, "one of the gods up in the sky threw down a baobab tree from his garden. It landed upside down on Earth but still continued to grow."

That is why the tree's branches look like a set of upside-down roots.

There is something for everyone in the baobab tree, whether man, woman, boy, or girl. Something for beasts and spirits, even.

Papa places the empty fruit gourds in different corners of our house to chase away lizards and snakes.

Mama cooks Papa's favorite *miyan kuka* soup with the baobab's leaves.

My oldest brother, Abraham, squeezes powder from the

dried fruit gourds onto the pimples on his face. My second brother, Elijah, squeezes powder from the dried fruit gourds into the boil on his leg. My third brother, Caleb, uses the empty pods to store his shaving stick.

Men and boys gather under the upside-down branches of the baobab tree in front of our village health care center, exchanging news or deciding who to vote for in the next election.

Women and girls gather under the baobab tree near the communal well, exchanging gossip or deciding what styles of clothes to sew next.

Goats and sheep take refuge from the heat under the baobab tree; bats and owls sleep in its branches; animals chomp on the baobab's trunk during the dry season, eager for the volumes of water stored inside its bark.

Some of the students in my class whose fathers are hunters say that drinks made from soaking the baobab fruit in water would protect you from being gobbled up by crocodiles. They say that plucking the flowers, which normally fall to the ground on their own within hours of blooming, would lead to your being torn apart by lions.

But Pastor Moses says that drying the leaves and firing them up as incense would not drive out demons and witches from your house or prevent evil spirits from disturbing you and your family.

"It's all superstition," he says. "Only God can deliver you from demons and witches, and from every other evil."

Sarah crouches on the ground beneath the baobab tree while I slip off my rubber sandals and stand on her back, then grab as many of the hairy, egg-shaped fruits as my fingers can clutch. One day, I shall be as tall as Mama and will need neither my friend's back nor a long stick to reach my favorite fruits.

PAPA'S RADIO

FROM THE MOMENT HE arises at dawn till he pats my head softly with his rough hand and retires after dusk, the voices go on and on; transmitting stories from other worlds strange and inconceivable to our own real world, but in the Hausa language that we speak.

Every three weeks or so, Jacob can be certain of two new batteries to dismember or bandy in the backyard. But, whenever he can afford it, Papa buys the kind of batteries that can last up to six weeks, at least.

Papa's small black radio follows him with his hoe and machete to the farm. It keeps him company in the living room while he awaits Mama's cooking. It stands by his side when he lounges under the baobab tree, in need of siesta or shade.

Papa's radio never stops talking, whether perched on a ledge or on a mat or between his ear and shoulder: "You are listening to BBC Hausa, brought to you live from our studios in London."

The radio keeps silent only after the door to Papa's bedroom groans shut at night. The voices sleep only when Papa himself sleeps.

"We will have to put it in the grave with him when he dies," Mama jokes. "Otherwise, he will come back and haunt all of us."

THANK GOD

"WE MUST ALWAYS FIND reasons to thank God," Mama says. "Everything happens for a reason."

That was what she said when her third baby died of a fever when he was four years old, strapped to Mama's back on the twenty-minute walk to the village health care center.

That was what she said when her fourth baby died of a fever when she was one year old, suckling Mama's breast one minute and lifeless the next.

That was what she said when her seventh baby was born dead, its body swaddled in worn cloth by the toothless midwife and made to disappear, no opportunity given to me for even a peek.

That was what she said when her ninth child turned out to be yet another boy, after she had prayed hard for one more girl.

"Thank God, because it is better to have more boys than one boy and many girls," she said. "Or worse, to have no boys at all."

Like Mama, I also am learning to be thankful.

Five brothers means five extra plates to wash up after breakfast and dinner, and five extra sets of laundry to tackle in the backyard every Saturday.

But it also means five pairs of hands to sow seeds and reap crops.

And a steady supply of food and labor when Papa becomes too old and too tired to till the soil.

And five future brides who will give birth to five batches of sons and daughters.

And wives who will cook and clean and make sure that Papa and Mama are well taken care of long after I have gone away to help take care of my own husband's father and mother.

And, even though Abraham is running a temperature and can't join Papa at the farm today, my immediate older brother, Isaac, is the one who forfeits attending school, not me. To ensure that all clearing and plowing is completed on schedule, Isaac exchanges his notebooks for a hoe and cutlass, while I am free to go and learn.

I thank God for Papa.

Unlike many other girls in our village whose parents do not think that sending a girl to school is important since she will end up getting married and taking all her father's years of investment to another man's house, Papa wants me educated.

He wants me to grow up and be like the women wearing white coats in the Maiduguri General Hospital, or like those he hears on his radio discussing important topics, or like those who come to our church from time to time to talk to the congregation about the importance of sending girls to school.

YA TA

"YA TA, BRING SOME Vaseline for my hands," Papa says after he rinses the soil from his fingernails.

"Ya Ta, come and help me comb my hair," Mama says after she loosens the previous week's plaits.

"Ya Ta, bring a razor blade and trim my toenail," Papa says when his little toe has once again grown a coarse stub.

"Ya Ta, come and help me zip up my blouse," Mama says when she is on her way to attend a meeting for all the women in Christ the King Church.

Papa and Mama have only one daughter. Nobody else for them to assign special tasks but me.

Nobody else who will hear them call "Ya Ta" and come running, nobody else who is "my daughter" to them.

THE VOICE ON PAPA'S RADIO

"AND NOW, FROM BBC Hausa, here are some of the top stories from around the world:

"Huge waves have battered the southern and western coasts of the UK, as forecasters warn exposed areas could see a fresh round of flooding. Waves of up to eight meters were recorded off Land's End, Cornwall. The environment secretary said seven people have died and seventeen hundred homes have been flooded in England due to storms. There are currently three severe flood warnings in place in England and travel by road and rail is being hit.

"Nigerian movie star Omotola J. Ekeinde, known to her fans as Omosexy, has told the BBC she doesn't wear makeup at home and pounds her own yam, a food staple in Nigeria. The Nollywood actress was named as one of *Time* magazine's one hundred most influential people in the world in 2013."

CALENDAR

I FLIP THE BACK cover of my English exercise book and check the calendar I drew on it with blue ink.

Only fifteen days since the top students in our school took the Borno State scholarship exam for exceptional children from disadvantaged homes.

Obviously too early to expect any news about our results.

STORYTELLER

"THEY WERE SHOOTING FROM atop motorbikes and throwing grenades," Danladi says, gesticulating wildly with his arms and legs.

The entire class is gathered around his desk, listening to his secondhand tale about a shootout between the police and Boko Haram men right in the middle of a street in Damboa, witnessed by his older brother who lives there.

"Everywhere, there was fire and smoke," he says, adding a deafening "boom!"

"But how did your brother manage to see it all?" I ask. "Wasn't he afraid that he would get shot?"

"People were jumping into gutters and hiding behind trees," he replies. "My brother climbed on top of a roof."

Sometimes, it is difficult to know which of Danladi's stories are true and which are exaggerated or fabricated.

FAT FISH

A DELICIOUS NIGHT OF *miyan kuka* with fat portions of fish, chunkier than a three-year-old's fist. Mama serves my brothers the segments around the fin, while I get the tail.

I imagine the clueless creature flapping in happy haste through Lake Chad, which borders Borno State, unaware that its destiny is a pot of soup hundreds of kilometers away.

I imagine the angler, pleased with the day's catch, eager for the traders who will travel from far and wide to purchase his ill-fated fish.

If only we had our own freshwater nearby. If only Mama could make more dinners with fish as fat and scrumptious as this.

At the end, nothing but fingerprints are left over in my enamel bowl. Not even the long, thin bones of the *banda* are spared.

And there's just enough remnant in Mama's pot for a repeat session tomorrow.

"Ya Ta, make sure you cover the pot properly," Mama says, "so that no rat will climb inside."

SLEEP

MY MOUTH EXPELS ONE loud yawn after another. My mind seems covered in mist. My eyelids, too heavy, flutter nonstop.

My body is begging for sleep.

But there are five more pages left in chapter four of my social studies textbook.

I must read about the three main ethnic groups in Nigeria, their different modes of dress and choices of food. I must learn in which of the thirty-six states of the country they reside. I must learn how to say "good morning," "good afternoon," and "good evening" in each of their languages.

I must be ready for Malam Zwindila.

Hausa, we all already know, of course, which means that his test questions will most likely be about the Igbo and Yoruba ethnic groups.

Weary from my battle with sleep, I rise from Mama's stool on the veranda and head to the backyard. Careful not to startle my slumbering family, I select one basin from Mama's stack of enamelware.

I fill the basin with water and set it by the stool. I dip my feet inside and resume reading.

Impossible for sleep to come upon me when my bare soles are freezing cold in water.

RAT BITE

Jacob wakes up weeping.

"My hand! My hand!" he wails.

My five-year-old brother sheds tears of a stricken thief. The fresh teeth marks on his outstretched hand are the most damning clue.

Each nibble of a rat's teeth is usually followed by a blast of air from its tiny mouth, a smart trick the rodent must have been taught by its mother. In your sleep, you hope the cool, refreshing waft will never stop. You believe God has blessed you with a fan.

It is not until you wake that you realize exactly what damage the rat has done. I know from harrowing experience.

By then, the creature and its cool blast are gone, leaving you with the sharp pain and the dried blood and the raw wounds.

My other brothers would have paid dearly. I would have marched straight to Papa and reported the crime.

But I cannot bear to see Jacob's budding genitals smeared with fresh pepper.

Or hear his shrill yelps of pain.

Or watch my sweet little brother, whom I have bathed, cuddled, and nestled since the day he belted his first cry, given the punishment meant for a thief—for a child who lifted the lid and pinched a chunk of fish from his mother's pot of soup, ate his booty in bed but neglected to wash his hand before falling asleep. The rat must have mistaken his soiled fingers for a piece of fish.

"Don't worry," I say. "I won't tell Papa. Come, let me put some Vaseline on your hand."

He sniffles and clinches my thighs.

THE VOICE ON PAPA'S RADIO

"THE NOMINATIONS FOR THIS year's Academy Awards have been announced in Los Angeles. *American Hustle, 12 Years a Slave, Gravity, Philomena,* and *Her* are just some of the films vying for the best picture award. The announcement for best picture nominees was made by actor Chris Hemsworth, alongside Oscars chief Cheryl Boone Isaacs.

"Fifty-five people have been killed in the northeast of Nigeria in coordinated attacks by the Boko Haram militant group, the Nigerian army said. It said one hundred and five prisoners were freed in the predawn raid in Bama, Borno State. Bama's police station, military barracks, and government buildings were burned to the ground, said the military and witnesses."

PRINCIPAL

"MY FATHER HAS SEEN many white people before," Danladi says, "not just on TV but in real life."

According to him, his father met the white people when he was a child, back when part of the Sambisa forest—which stretches all the way from Borno to Yobe, Gombe, and Bauchi States in northeast Nigeria, and even up to Jigawa and Kano States in the northwest—was a game reserve.

"He said many white people from faraway lands often came to look at the animals," Danladi says. "They were never tired of taking photos."

I have never seen a white person in real life, but everybody says that our school principal is a white man, never mind that his skin is black.

He never speaks to his students in Hausa, unless our parents are nearby so that they can understand. English rolls off his tongue swiftly and smoothly, as if the words are coated in melted butter.

He wears shiny black shoes and buttoned shirts tucked into belted trousers, instead of open-toe sandals or flowing caftans. His clothes and footwear are never speckled, not even during the harmattan season when a ferocious wind blows a steady swarm of dust from the Sahara Desert.

He uses methods less strenuous than the koboko to compel naughty students to plead guilty. "Why have I sent for you?" he asks at the beginning of the encounter, and in nine cases out of ten, the child addressed, paralyzed by nervousness, confesses everything.

He never attends occasions in the village, not even church or mosque, traveling to Maiduguri almost every other day to be with a family we suspect exists but have never seen.

He lines the walls of his narrow office with books, some thin, some thick, some too soft to stand in the shelves. Students swear that he has read every single one at least twice.

"But no white tourist can dare approach the Sambisa forest now," Danladi says. "That's where all the Boko Haram people go to hide from the soldiers and the police."

SITTING ON A WOODEN STOOL

SARAH PLAITS MY THICK strands into thin cornrows, the ends drooping over my ears and around the back of my head.

I plait Sarah's soft strands into thin cornrows, the ends drooping over her jaw and around the back of her neck.

ROMANCE

On the veranda in Aisha's house, her husband's head is bowed toward the Muslim holy city of Mecca, his feet bare on a turquoise mat.

Maybe he sees us, maybe he is too absorbed to notice. We creep past Malam Isa without extending any greeting, careful not to disturb his prayers.

As usual, Aisha wants to hear everything that happened in school from Monday to Friday: who got whipped by the koboko, who answered the most questions, who taught anything new in their subject.

Sometimes, I bring my notebooks for Aisha to study. Sarah never bothers to bring hers because nobody else but me can decipher her handwriting. Her *I*s look like *J*s, her *K*s look like *X*s, her *R*s look like *P*s.

"So, what's the difference between democracy and other types of government?" Aisha asks.

"It's there," I say. "I wrote down the definitions."

"Yes, I've read them. But I still don't understand the difference. If we vote for the leader in a military government, is it still a democracy?"

"Mmmmmm," Sarah says.

The Monday after Aisha's wedding to Malam Isa at the village mosque, Sarah and I arrived in school with the flower and spirogyra patterns painted on all the bride's friends still glistening on our arms and feet. But Aisha did not turn up.

Her father-in-law was worried that an educated wife would be less likely to abide by the wishes of her husband and in-laws. Like many other Muslim and Christian brides in our school, Aisha has never been back to the classroom since her wedding.

But Aisha has not changed much since her days in school with us. Her questions were rarely straightforward, sometimes difficult, and often many, even more than Malam Zwindila himself could ask.

"The difference between a democracy and a military government is like a monkey and a gorilla," I say.

She adjusts her hijab and perks up her ears.

"When a monkey comes into the farm to steal bananas, the farmer can chase the monkey and it will run away. But if a gorilla comes to the farm to steal bananas, if the farmer tries to chase it away, the gorilla can decide to not just steal all the bananas, but to also kill the farmer."

Aisha's eyes are transfixed on me. Sarah's eyes stray to the carton of DVDs beside the bed.

"The monkey is like the government of the people in a democracy while the gorilla is like a military government."

"Ah, I see," she says.

But Sarah and I are not here just to talk with Aisha. We are here to watch films.

A week after their wedding, Malam Isa bought Aisha a TV

and DVD player. He allows her to keep them in the room beside their bedroom where she will stay with their baby after it is born. No one to tell her what she can and cannot watch. No one to change the channel when she wants to know who died next. Not even his sisters can touch the TV without Aisha's permission. I have never known a man who cared so much for his wife.

"I want a love story," Sarah says.

"No, let's watch an adventure," I say.

"No, a love story. Pleeeease. We can watch an adventure after."

Will there be enough time to watch a love story and then an adventure before it is time to go home and help Mama with the evening meal?

Sarah slots in one of the romance films where the actors and actresses speak nothing but Hausa.

ONCE A MONTH

"WHY HAVEN'T YOU BEEN in school?" Malam Zwindila asks.

"I was sick with malaria," I reply.

"I hope you're feeling better," he says.

Sometimes, I wonder if Malam Zwindila suspects.

Last month, it was a running stomach. The month before, it was a fever. The month before that, I told him I was ill with a splitting headache. I wonder if Malam Zwindila is fooled by my lies, and by those of Sarah, and most likely other girls in my class, too.

Like lending my pen to Danladi, who always chews off the cap by the time he finally hands it back, going to school when I am on my period is something I decided to never do again.

Within the first few hours of sitting in class, my carefully folded piece of cloth is usually soaked through, defenseless against the flow of blood.

The school's only toilet is in Principal's office. But he keeps it under lock and key—too many students dirtied it.

The nearby bushes have no water. Nowhere for me to dash in between classes and swap my soaked sanitary cloth for another, or to rinse my used ones.

During last term's English language exam, my mind swung from the questions in front of me to my drenched underwear.

When it was over, I didn't bother to wait for Sarah. I went straight home with my exercise books shielding the stain.

Everyone must have wondered why I had my two hands at my backside, walking like a principal inspecting rows of students to ensure that none was barefoot instead of wearing sandals. All the way home, I felt as if the ground should suddenly cave in beneath my feet and cover up after I had dropped inside.

But I was lucky.

Rifkatu stood up to answer a question in class last month, unaware that her dress was soiled. Everyone stared. Some boys giggled.

She has not been back in school since.

PASTOR MOSES

As the woman with the light mustache leads the entire congregation of Christ the King Church in praise and worship to God, my eyes wander from pew to pew. Her daughter, Magdalene, who is a class ahead of me in school, was also chosen to sit for the scholarship exam.

With each fresh song she raises, my voice sings, my hands clap, my waist jiggles. But my mind is searching.

Searching for someone special.

After we are hoarse from singing and drenched from dancing, Pastor Moses mounts the stage. He stands quietly for a while, then clears his throat and begins his sermon.

"Our scripture reading is taken from the book of James, chapter one, verse two. And I read: 'My brethren, count it all joy when you fall into various trials.'"

Those in the congregation who are literate, those who can afford Bibles, those who received free Bibles from the Believers' LoveWorld evangelists that visited our village last Christmas, turn to the prescribed chapter and follow his words with their eyes. The rest look at his lips and listen.

Sarah believes that her father's goat must have consumed her own free Bible when she forgot it on their veranda after church two Sundays ago, so I shift closer to her and place mine open on our laps.

"As a Christian, you have Jesus Christ living in you," Pastor Moses says. "This makes you a victor in life, irrespective of what you pass through. You're unconquerable. Every challenge you pass through is just a springboard to your next level of glory, no matter how dire the situation."

My eyes resume their wandering.

Maybe I missed him. Maybe he came in late. Maybe he is standing at the back of the long hall as he sometimes does.

Maybe Pastor Moses's son, Success, is home from university. Maybe this is one of the weekends when he travels all the way from Maiduguri to visit his father and mother.

Maybe the powder and eyeliner I borrowed from Mama will not be a waste. Maybe the white shoes Sarah lent me will not be in vain.

ON OUR WAY TO SCHOOL

"Success hasn't visited in quite a while," I say. "I hope he's well."

Sarah giggles, and shoves me sideways with her waist.

"The loving doe and the graceful deer!"

"Shush," I whisper, clapping my hand to her mouth.

But I also giggle. I know that my secret is safe with her.

TALES BY MOONLIGHT

HARDLY ANYONE HAS TIME for fun and games when the farm is uppermost on our minds.

No time to climb the surrounding hills and play hide-and-seek among the rocks.

But, after the months of preparing and planting, after the year's yield has been gathered and stored, then the entertainment galore can begin. Until then, life remains routine.

But there is always time for a folktale by moonlight.

Together with my brothers and the neighbors' children, I sit on a mat spread out in front of our house.

"Story, story," Papa says.

"Story!" we reply.

"There was a king who had three children," Papa begins. "One day, he decided to test which was the most skilled among them, to know who would take over after he died."

The king asked his sons to mount their horses and follow him to a baobab tree. There, they would display their different skills and then he would decide.

The first son galloped at top speed and thrust his spear into the baobab tree. It pierced right through, from one side to the other.

"The hole was so large that he rode through it with his

horse," Papa says. "And then, it was the turn of the second son."

Like his brother before him, he galloped toward the baobab tree at top speed, then jumped right over it with his horse.

As for the third son, he rode toward the baobab tree and uprooted it with his bare hands while still sitting on the back of his horse, then waved the tree at his father.

"Now, which of these three do you think is the greatest?" Papa asks.

On and on, all of us boys and girls debate this for the rest of the night.

ALMOST ONE MONTH

NEWS OF OUR EXAM results will most likely come soon.

BLOOD

THROUGH THE WINDOWS OF the classroom, our eyes follow the pink van as it drives into the school premises and parks in front of Principal's office. We titter in excitement.

A pink van, blue van, red van, green van, or van of any color driving into our school usually means something new and free.

One time, people in a blue van gave each child a mosquito net. Inscribed on the packet were the words "Kick Malaria Out of Africa, One Mosquito at a Time—courtesy of the Bill and Melinda Gates Foundation." Another time, a green van brought exercise books and pens, "courtesy of the Rotary Club of Maiduguri." Yet another time, a brown van brought cholera medication from the federal ministry of health.

What might the van have brought this time?

The mystery thickens when the boys are instructed to hurry home after school. Reluctantly, they pack their books and gaze longingly at the pink van as they shuffle out, while the girls happily wait behind.

My anticipation swells.

Even Principal is nowhere in sight as a tall, thin woman with long braids gathers us around her van and starts speaking.

It is the first time I have heard anyone discuss menstruation in a loud voice. And she looks us straight in the eye while she speaks!

Shrinking with shame, I search for somewhere to hide my face.

This is a conversation for hushed tones.

This is a topic reserved for mothers and daughters.

Apart from Mama—and Sarah—nobody else knows my secret. My fresh rags are well hidden in a plastic bag stuffed deep inside Mama's bag of blouses and wrappers. My soaked rags go straight into a bucket of soapy water. I hang them out to dry only after Papa and my brothers have gone to sleep. Before they awake, I grab the damp rags from the clothesline.

"As growing girls, your bodies are changing," the woman says. "That should not make you afraid. It should also not make you feel ashamed. It's normal. Every woman goes through the same changes. Most especially, it should not mean you have to miss school. You don't have to miss classes because of the changes in your body."

Another one of my secrets. But how does this woman know?

From inside her pink van, she extracts a pink packet and gives one to each of us. "Courtesy of Operation Keep a Girl in School," the inscription reads. Then she unseals one of the pink packets and tells us what to do with the contents.

Can her words be true?

It is difficult to believe that these spotless white pads, pristine and fragrant as the pages of a new book, are for something so disgraceful and dirty.

HUNGER

ONCE AGAIN, I STEP out onto the veranda and peer into the horizon. No sign of Mama.

My hunger twists and turns and bites and barks. Why is she late returning home from the market?

And then her vast raffia basket comes into view!

It is balanced on her head with her two hands stretched upward to keep it straight. Mama's pace is long and brisk, almost a sprint. I run to meet her.

No matter how much or how little Papa gives for the mid-week shopping, there is always something extra in Mama's basket—*dabino* or *kuli kuli*—to temporarily silence my hunger while she sets about preparing the evening meal.

TEACHER

"WHAT DAY IS TODAY?" Jacob asks.

"Today is Thursday," I reply.

"What day is tomorrow?"

"Tomorrow is Friday."

"Is tomorrow always Friday?"

"No."

I mark off each day of the week, finger after finger.

"Thursday's tomorrow is Friday," I say. "Friday's tomorrow is Saturday, then Sunday, Monday, Tuesday, Wednesday, and Wednesday's tomorrow is Thursday."

"But you just said today is Thursday," he says. "If today is Thursday, then how come Thursday is tomorrow?"

Ha ha.

Jacob.

He will make a clever pupil someday if God provides Papa with enough to allow him to start school.

For now, all he wants to know is which particular tomorrow I intend to continue from where I stopped and teach him how to write the English alphabet from M to Z.

PEPPER SOUP

THE STRONG SCENT OF boiled goat meat brings warm saliva to my mouth as we approach Aisha's house. She always alerts Sarah and me a day in advance, whenever her husband decides to slaughter one of his goats.

No one in the world makes goat-meat pepper soup as scrumptious as Aisha's—not even Mama, I'm sorry to say. Malam Isa's friends probably know this as well, which must be why they never turn down the invitation from him.

"Good evening," Sarah and I say.

"Good evening," they reply.

Seated with Malam Isa on the veranda are Malam Emmanuel, who sometimes handles the Bible study lessons in our church when Pastor Moses is away, and Malam Shettima, who teaches Islamiya classes to Muslim boys and girls on Sunday afternoons.

A bowl of pepper soup is set on a stool in their midst, chunks of goat meat protruding on the surface. One after the other, they dip their spoons into the steaming delicacy, then make long hissing noises as they swallow the hot fluid with care before beginning to chew.

"Tell Aisha to bring some more drinking water for me," Malam Emmanuel says as Sarah and I walk past them and into the house.

"Okay," we reply.

"Or would you prefer *zobo*?" Malam Isa asks. "It's fresh."

Malam Emmanuel nods.

"I think that will be better," he says.

"Tell Aisha to bring the keg of *zobo* in my room," Malam Isa says. "The one my sister sent today."

Sarah and I hurry along, eager for our own share of the soup. And, if we are lucky, there may be some *zobo* left over for us as well.

THE VOICE ON PAPA'S RADIO

"US PRESIDENT BARACK OBAMA has vowed to make 2014 'a year of action' in his annual State of the Union address to Congress. He pledged to bypass Congress if necessary to tackle economic inequality and raise the minimum wage. On foreign policy, Mr. Obama urged Congress to close Guantanamo Bay prison in the next twelve months and threatened to veto any sanctions bill on Iran.

"A car bomb has exploded in the northeastern Nigerian city of Maiduguri, killing at least seventeen people. The Islamist group Boko Haram said it carried out the attack. A suspect has been arrested, the military says. The bomb went off near a market, sending up a large plume of smoke. People were seen fleeing the scene covered in blood. The immediate aftermath of the blast was described as chaotic, with bodies on the ground and troops firing automatic weapons."

Maiduguri.

I pray that Success is safe.

I pray that Principal's family is safe.

I pray that the special school for girls, and all the teachers, students, and buildings are safe.

I pray that I will soon find security for my future within the school's four walls.

SUCCESS

As soon as Pastor Moses concludes the closing prayer, a commotion ensues.

Like fowls in a farm when the grain chaff is scattered, out we all come rushing toward the back of the hall, bewitched by the bright colors leaping up and down on Success's laptop screen.

Whenever he travels from Maiduguri to visit his parents, Success brings his laptop along with him to church. As soon as the Sunday morning service is over, he leaves it open for us on a wooden bench at the back of the hall.

Sometimes we watch Jesus in cartoons; sometimes we watch Pharaoh drowning in the Red Sea or Jonah being swallowed by a fish; sometimes we watch a pitch-black screen with an orange triangle in the middle, while a deep, strong voice that sounds like God's renders different chapters of the Bible.

Success told me that there is nothing you cannot do with a laptop.

You can use it to send messages to people in other parts of the world. You can use it as both your TV and your telephone. You can write page after page of social studies and science notes on it, without your parents worrying about you being sent out of class halfway through the school day because they did not have enough money to buy you new exercise books.

Apart from telling me about his laptop, he has told me all I wanted to know about his university. And about his law degree. He has told me about his journey from Maiduguri to Kano, and about his plans to visit the megacity of Lagos one of these days. He has told me that the Bible is not only written in English; there are Hausa and Igbo and Yoruba versions, and even Arabic, which is the same language in which Malam Isa's Quran is written.

What else is there to ask him about?

What other question will keep him by my side until his father is done with the long queue of church members waiting to see their pastor?

What other excuse will let me stand alone with him while the other children remain with the laptop?

Next thing I know, Success is standing by my side. He is the one who has a question for me!

"Have you read any new books recently?" he asks.

I jitter.

I am about to fall to the ground and faint.

"Books? Yes, I'm already in chapter ten of my social studies textbook."

"No, no. I mean storybooks. Have you read any books other than your textbooks?"

"Oh."

Papa and Mama can barely afford school fees and textbooks. Apart from *Eze Goes to School* and *Drummer Boy*, which we read as part of our English class, the only storybook I own is *The Pied Piper of Hamelin*. When I made the highest overall score after last year's exams, Principal gave it to me.

I must have read it from cover to cover two hundred times before I finally lent it to Aisha, who then lent it to her sister-in-law, who had also dropped out of school.

The girl's husband saw her reading it, engrossed while the dinner was burning in the pot. He lost his temper and flung my book straight into the cooking fire.

"I read a book called *Pied Piper of Hamelin*," I reply. "It's about a town that was invaded by rats. So the people hired a man who could play mysterious songs. The rats heard him playing one of his songs and came running out of their holes, and followed him until he led them to the river and they all jumped inside and drowned."

"That sounds very interesting," Success says. "I haven't read it before."

My balloon bursts. Now, we will have nothing else to talk about.

"But I have lots of other interesting storybooks," he continues. "I'll bring some for you when I visit next," he says. "There's this series about a girl, a girl just like you, who goes about solving mysteries. Her name is Nancy Drew. I'll bring some for you and after you finish reading them you can tell me what you think."

This is most certainly the best day of my life. Could this really be happening to me?

"Thank you."

I smile.

BEWITCHED

THE SOUND OF HIS name to my ears is like the smell of fried chicken to my nose.

Like a baobab tree among the trees of the forest, so is he among all the young men in the world. I delight to sit in his shade, and his alone, and his fruit is sweet to my taste.

Sweet, soft, smart, charming, tall, handsome, neat, strong, kind, reliable.

He is like a medical doctor, a school principal, an expert farmer, and a champion wrestler rolled into one.

His eyes are bright as the full moon in the sky. They shine with intelligence. They sparkle with mirth.

They bewitch me each time I am under their gaze.

MARRIAGE

It is my turn to crouch on the sand while Sarah plants her feet on my back and reaches into the branches of the baobab tree. As the first of the hard green fruits drops from her hand to the ground, I scream.

"Be careful!"

"Sorry!" she says. "Are you okay?"

"I'm fine. Don't worry, it didn't hit me. It just fell too close to my head."

"Ah. I'd better be more careful. What will I tell Success if I crack his wife's head open?"

"Shhhhhhhhh!"

Her laughter causes me to wobble. My wobbling forces my palms deeper into the soil. I'm in a tizzy at the thought of being married to Success.

Although marriage is the last thing on my mind for now.

Marriage means a husband who will want his breakfast at dawn and his feet massaged at dusk. Marriage means babies who will need breast milk and bathing and beatings to teach them how to behave as they grow. Marriage means little time left over to stay awake and study books at the end of each day.

But would Success want to marry me?

Chatting in the church hall is one thing. Walking down

the aisle and saying "I do" is another altogether.

Would Success be interested in marrying a girl with no university degree? For the billionth time, I say a silent prayer for that Borno State government scholarship.

I want to attend the special boarding school for girls in Maiduguri. I want to go to university and get a degree. I want to be a teacher and impart everything I know to other children like Jacob. I want to travel to the places I hear about from Malam Zwindila and from Papa's radio, countries in faraway corners of the world.

When six large baobab fruits are lying on the ground around me, Sarah hops down and gathers them in her arms, while I stand and dust my knees.

NEWS FROM IZGHE

ABRAHAM RUSHES THROUGH THE raffia gate that leads into our backyard, panting, as if a police officer is chasing him.

Excitement shines through every pore and pimple on his face.

"It rained in Izghe two days ago!" he announces in the veranda. "It rained in Izghe at night!"

"Really?" Papa shouts from behind the corrugated iron partition that hides our toilet and bathroom from the rest of the backyard.

"It's true," Abraham replies. "I just heard from my friend who came in from there this morning. It looks as if the rains will be early this year."

"Thank God!"

"Wonderful!"

"Great news!"

Rejoicing, Mama, my brothers, and I jump up and clap our hands. In his haste to join us, Papa forgets to replace the iron sheet on his way out of the enclosure.

He must also have forgotten to replace the plastic cover for the deep hole in the ground. The faint scent of feces floats from our pit toilet into the veranda.

"This is very good news!" Papa says. "Very good news indeed!"

Izghe is just about 190 kilometers from our village. Like us, they suffered late rains last year, so the planting had to be postponed from April to July.

The corn and groundnut seeds ended up in the mounds at a time when we should have been planting beans. The beans went into the ridges at a time when we should have been harvesting corn. The harvest extended into a season when we should all have been resting at home or attending wrestling matches and Bible quiz competitions.

In the meantime, each new morning brought terrifying thoughts of starving or borrowing or begging, as the previous year's harvest depleted day by day.

Papa considered going to Maiduguri to find work as a cleaner or a laborer.

Mama knelt down and prayed for an hour before bed night after night.

I worried that there may be no money to pay my fees for the next term, that I would be forced to drop out of school.

Thank God that the rains have come early to Izghe. If it has happened in Izghe, then it will surely happen to us.

EVIL

TODAY'S CHURCH SERVICE IS different. Pastor Moses does not follow the regular program. Instead of launching into his sermon right after the praise and worship by Magdalene's mother, he asks us all to stand and pray.

"Let us lift our voices in prayer for our brothers and sisters in other parts of Borno State who are being killed by Boko Haram," he says. "Let us pray that God will deliver them from this evil."

Men, women, boys, and girls raise their voices to God, a cacophony of pleas and heartfelt requests.

Sometimes, I wonder about Boko Haram. They want a new country, governed by Islamic laws. At first, they were known by their Arabic name, Jama'atu Ahlis Sunna Lidda'awati wal-Jihad, "People Committed to the Propagation of the Prophet's Teachings and Jihad." But their hatred of education led residents of Maiduguri to start calling them by a Hausa name, Boko Haram, "Western education is forbidden."

But Aisha told me that the Islam of Boko Haram is different from the one that she and Malam Isa practice.

"Their Islam is from inside their heads, not from the holy Quran," she said.

For the past few years, Boko Haram has been attacking

police stations and other government buildings in Maiduguri, and also bombing churches in major cities. More recently, they have been attacking villages and towns.

"Dear Lord Jesus," Pastor Moses says, "we ask that You protect our brothers and sisters all over Borno State from Boko Haram. We ask that You send angels to watch over them and to keep them safe from harm. Please, deliver them from this present darkness. Let evil not prevail in our land, in Jesus's name we pray!"

"Amen!"

"WHO IS SO UGLY that he only comes out at night?" I ask.

"The bat!" Sarah replies. "Who beats a child up right in front of the child's mother?" Sarah asks.

"Hunger!" I reply.

"Who does the whole world fear; he doesn't know mother from father, he can't tell rich from poor, or strong from weak, he wakes you up when your sleep is sweetest?" I ask.

"Death," Sarah replies.

FOUR LOAVES OF BREAD

THE WOMAN IN THE pink van was not exaggerating. The pads in the pink packet protect like magic!

But each packet will cost Mama the same as four loaves of bread.

"I see them for sale in the big markets," Mama says.

In that case, I had better save the remaining five pads for a more critical time, someday when we are writing tests or exams.

I pray that I will see the woman in the pink van again someday.

LOVE

"THIS BABY IS GOING to be a boy," Aisha says. "Just look at how vigorously he kicks!"

I touch Aisha's belly with my right hand. Kick, kick, almost as mild as a heartbeat. Sarah remains transfixed, eyes and ears sold out to the love story playing on the TV screen; the groom whispers into the ears of his bride, and a smile lights up her eyes.

"Have you heard anything about the scholarship?" Aisha asks.

I sigh. "Not yet."

"I'm sure you'll pass," she says. "If you don't, I don't know who else will."

But other contenders from all over Borno State were also the best female students in their own classes. Maybe my intelligence was just a monitor among lizards, while that of other competing students was an alligator or crocodile.

"Just look at how much she loves him," Sarah says, her eyes still transfixed by the screen.

The wife in the romance film serves her husband's breakfast on her knees. She picks his teeth after he is done with his meal. She sees him to the door as he heads out to work. She slips his shoes off his feet when he returns.

He hands her a pretty package that contains a glittering gold necklace that he adjusts around her neck. She beams.

"I want to love my husband like that," Sarah says, her eyes twinkling like midnight stars.

ANOTHER HUSBAND

PASTOR MOSES DOES NOT exit the stage after his sermon.

While the offering basket is traveling from hand to hand and pew to pew, he hovers by the lectern, grinning from ear to ear.

"This morning, I have a very special announcement to make," he says. "God is blessing my family with a new addition. My son is getting married."

My heart crashes. My face sinks. My world ends.

Maybe Success would have waited if I'd been granted the government scholarship, if he knew that I would be attending the special school in Maiduguri and then certainly going on to university afterward.

The rest of the congregation claps.

"The wedding will take place in Jalingo," Pastor Moses continues. "You are all welcome to attend. I have asked Emmanuel to commence the travel arrangements. Please, put down your name with him at the end of the service, so that we know exactly how many to plan for."

I remain sitting in my pew while the church rises at the close of service. Sarah takes one look at me and resumes her place by my side.

Together, we watch almost all the mothers in church gather

around Malam Emmanuel, including Mama. The fathers know that wedding jollification is mostly a women's affair, and that Pastor Moses's wife will need as many hands as possible with the cooking and serving of guests.

Sarah clasps my hand and massages my fingers. But her attempts to comfort me do little to soothe my broken heart.

Success promised to bring me storybooks. Now I may never get to read about the girl like me who goes about solving mysteries.

"Don't worry," Sarah says. "God will find you another husband."

PROSPER

IT TURNS OUT THAT all my heartbreak is for nothing. Pastor Moses's oldest son, Prosper, is the one getting married.

"Because of his job, he hardly comes home," Sarah says. "He works in the general hospital in Jalingo."

"Are you sure?" I ask.

"That's what my mother told me."

"Is she sure?"

"That's what Malam Emmanuel told her. She said the woman Prosper is marrying works in Jalingo as well."

Thank God.

Success still belongs to me.

THE VOICE ON PAPA'S RADIO

"DISNEY ANIMATION FROZEN HAS become the top-grossing animated film in box office history. The musical film has now made $1.072 billion globally, beating Toy Story 3's previous record of $1.063 billion in 2010. Frozen, loosely based on the Hans Christian Andersen fairy tale The Snow Queen, has made $398.4 million in North America plus $674 million at the global box office.

"About thirty-nine people are believed to have been killed in an attack by Islamist militants on a Nigerian town. Local residents said the attack on Konduga, in the northeast Borno State, lasted several hours, beginning shortly before sundown on Tuesday night with the arrival of gunmen in four-by-four trucks. A mosque and more than a thousand homes were razed to the ground, residents said. The region is a stronghold of Boko Haram that is waging an insurgency against the government. Konduga is thirty-five kilometers from the Borno State capital of Maiduguri. Boko Haram has been conducting a four-year campaign of violence to push for Islamic rule in northern Nigeria."

TOUCHING A BOY'S HAND

THE ROMANCE FILMS THAT Sarah and I watch with Aisha are usually similar to each other.

The main character is a boy whose parents must choose whom their son in the city should marry. They decide on a girl from the village who will make a good, obedient wife.

But there's a hitch.

Their educated son is in love with an educated girl from the city, and he wants to marry her instead.

The family is angry with their son's resistance. The boy is angry with his family's interference. A grand dispute ensues.

Always, the family wins.

The boy marries the village girl, but stays in touch with his true love from the city. Together, they go out to eat in places where meals are served on pretty tables in cozy corners; walk along the beach on sunny afternoons; sit on low fences and whisper into each other's ears.

As soon as the boy and girl reach out to hold hands, the scene cuts, the screen goes dark.

Not even Malam Isa, who loves his wife more than any man on TV ever can, disrespects our Hausa culture by holding a woman's hand in public.

But sometimes, I am tempted to ask Aisha questions about

what happens when the doors are closed, when no eyes are there to intrude.

I wonder how it feels to touch the hand of a boy who isn't my brother.

I wonder how it feels to hold Success's hand.

I wonder how Success would feel about me if I passed the scholarship exam and then went on to university just like him, and just like the true-love girl in the film.

HUMAN FLESH

No fish in tonight's *miyan kuka*. Papa gave Mama enough naira, but she was too afraid to buy it.

"Everyone in the market is afraid," she says.

They are afraid because the fish swimming in the basins of water in market stalls are all too large to be true, even larger than they were the other week. One *banda* alone could satisfy a family of five!

They worry that the fish might be feeding off the fat of the hundreds of corpses dumped into Lake Chad, people slaughtered by Boko Haram.

NAMING

IT IS EXACTLY EIGHT days since Malam Zwindila's wife gave birth to their first child. After school, we all troop to his house, merrily, like larks in a bright blue sky. Chairs with Christ the King Church etched into their plastic backs are lined up outside the thatched-roof house. Papa is already seated and so is Malam Isa.

Pastor Moses sits separately beside Malam Zwindila facing the crowd of chairs.

Sarah and I look around for Aisha. Sometimes, it is difficult to spot our friend among the other women and girls wearing hijabs. We find her on the back veranda, sitting on a straw mat with some other Muslim women.

As soon as Malam Zwindila's wife appears with her bundle of joy, Pastor Moses stands. All the aunts, uncles, friends, neighbors, and church members stop chattering. The naming ceremony begins with a prayer and a short sermon.

"You must choose your children's names carefully," Pastor Moses says. "A name can influence a person's behavior or circumstances. It can play a huge role in who or what your child becomes in life. Your child's name is your child's destiny."

Mrs. Zwindila, a scarf sitting high on her head and her arms weighed down with bangles, gives the sleeping infant to her beaming husband, who then passes the baby to Pastor Moses.

"What name have you chosen for your first child?" Pastor Moses asks.

For a change, someone else is doing the asking while Malam Zwindila is doing the answering.

"The child will be called Divine," Malam Zwindila announces with a smile.

"Praise the Lord!" the crowd chants.

When the clapping and rejoicing fizzles, Pastor Moses holds Divine up in his arms and prays.

"May Divine grow up to be as godlike as a human can possibly be. May God grant his parents the grace and wisdom to raise him up in the way he should go."

"Amen!"

Apart from relatives and wives, Malam Zwindila's students are the only children invited. The adults are served first, but the steaming *jollof* rice, laden with sliced onions and pepper, is worth the long wait.

I bite my piece of fried beef in half and save the larger piece for Jacob.

SWEET DREAM

"Congratulations!" Success says. "Of course, I already heard the news about your scholarship. I always knew you were a smart girl. Well done!"

As he reaches out to shake my hand, I awake.

"BUT WHAT COULD BE delaying the scholarship exam results?" I say. "I wonder if Principal knows."

"But he would have announced it by now if he knew anything." She pauses. "Maybe the results have been released but nobody from this village passed."

I feel as if I have been struck by a truck, as if I have been slapped awake from a sweet dream. But best friends must tell us the truth, no matter how painful.

Instantly, the mansions I have been building in the air collapse, the rubble forming a heap of quicksand at my feet.

"Don't worry," Sarah says. "Just pray that God will give your father enough money so that he can pay for your university by himself."

SARAH MUST BE RIGHT

I MIGHT AS WELL forget about it.

I might as well stop dreaming.

I might as well invest all my energy in praying so that Papa will continue to afford my secondary school fees, and then miraculously find the money to send me to university.

BAD MOOD

"Argh!" I scream.

Mama rushes from the kitchen, oil dripping from the ladle in her hand.

"Ya Ta, what's the matter?" she asks.

"Someone spilled water on my textbooks!"

"Is that why you're screaming like that?"

"These are the only books I have. If anything happens to them, Papa won't be able to buy me new ones."

Mama continues staring at me while I stomp toward the bedroom with my books.

Jacob jumps out of my way.

COME TO THINK OF IT

WHAT GAVE ME THE audacity to imagine that I would pass the scholarship exam, when no student from this village ever has?

THE VOICE ON PAPA'S RADIO

"Suspected Islamist militants have raided a Nigerian village and murdered dozens, according to witnesses. The gunmen reportedly rounded up a group of men in Izghe village and shot them, before going door to door and killing anyone they found."

Papa is in the bathroom. The splashing of water ceases.

Mama is in the kitchen. The scraping of spoon against pot halts.

I am on the veranda. The preoccupation with myself and my misery stops.

We are frozen, all of us, by the voice on Papa's radio.

Boko Haram is in Izghe.

GATHERED AROUND THE WELL

"THEY ARRIVE ON MOTORBIKES and shoot in the air," Musa, the welder's son, says as he draws his pail up from the hole with a rope.

"They slay all the men and boys while they make the women and girls disappear," Rosemary, the ice-block seller's daughter, says as she lowers her pail into the well.

They are talking about Boko Haram.

THE BOYS IN MY CLASS

"THEY BUILD BUNKERS UNDER the Sambisa forest," Danladi says. "When the soldiers come looking for them, they disappear into these bunkers."

"That's probably why the soldiers search and search but can't find them," Peter says, "no matter how hard they look."

"Some of them are disguised as cobblers or mobile manicurists, hiding explosives in their toolboxes, then detonating them in markets, schools, and churches," Ibrahim says.

They are talking about Boko Haram.

MY BROTHERS

"THEY USE CHARMS THAT make them appear and disappear," Abraham says.

"Many travelers have had their journeys cut short when men with bombs and guns suddenly appeared in the middle of the highway," Elijah says.

"They load goats, cows, donkeys, and camels with explosives, then send the livestock wandering into public places where they would detonate," Caleb says.

"That's how they bombed the markets in Banki and Bama," Isaac says. "And the market in Damboa."

They are talking about Boko Haram.

"A CHILD BORN TO any of them would automatically share its father's ideas and beliefs," Papa says. "It will grow up to kill, steal, and destroy.

"It doesn't matter whether the child knew or lived with its father. As long as it has the bad blood running through its veins, it will be the same."

He is talking about Boko Haram.

ON OUR WAY TO SCHOOL

"How do they make the women and girls disappear?" Sarah asks.

"Maybe it's magic. Maybe they use charms."

"But where do they go when they disappear?"

We are talking about Boko Haram.

MALAM ZWINDILA

"THEY CLAIM TO BE fighting to create an Islamic state in Nigeria," he says. "They don't believe in democracy. They plan to topple the government elected by Nigerians."

He laughs.

He marches to the chalkboard and draws a map of Nigeria, then shades a fraction at the top right.

"This is what the northeast of Nigeria looks like," he says. "Borno, Yobe, Adamawa, Bauchi, Gombe, Taraba . . . This is all of us. An insignificant portion when compared to the rest of Nigeria. And, yet, this army of bandits, who are just in Borno and some parts of Yobe and Adamawa, imagine that they can somehow take over the rest of the country, all the thirty-six states?" He laughs. "Lack of education really makes people stupid. How much more idiotic can they be?"

He is talking about Boko Haram.

THE VOICE ON PAPA'S RADIO

"THE NIGERIAN GOVERNMENT HAS come under a great deal of criticism over its handling of the Boko Haram menace. We are now joined by Nobel Prize winner Professor Wole Soyinka, the country's foremost writer and social commentator, to discuss why the government appears so helpless."

FEET IN COLD WATER

WHAT IF ALL THE legends surrounding Boko Haram are true? What happens to all the girls and women they cause to disappear? Do they end up in another world strange and new, or do they simply become nothing?

My mind abandons the textbook pages in my lap and travels to a different book.

The Pied Piper of Hamelin.

After the man in the strange long coat, half yellow and half red, lured all the rats into the river with his musical pipe, the leaders of the town refused to pay him his fees.

The Pied Piper became upset.

With the same pipe he used to entice the rats, he played another tune. And out poured all the children of Hamelin town.

Unable to move a step or cry, the parents and government officials watched as the Piper led their children to the mountainside. Suddenly, a wondrous portal opened and they disappeared inside.

When each was in to the very last, the mountainside shut fast.

And the children of Hamelin were never, ever seen again.

ISLAM

MALAM ISA AND HIS friends are gathered around Aisha's goat-meat pepper soup. But none of them dip their spoon into the bowl. They are too busy talking.

"Islam has always been a religion of peace," Malam Isa says, poking his finger at the air. "All Muslims are to love all and be just to all regardless of religion. The Quran makes that very clear. Prophet Muhammad himself lived peacefully with his Christian and Jewish neighbors."

"Exactly," Malam Shettima adds, swatting a fly from his face. "The Quran says, 'Let there be no compulsion in religion.'" He recites it in Arabic.

"Good evening," Sarah and I say on our way inside.

None of the men responds.

"Muslims are permitted to attack others only when we have been attacked. Only as a means of protecting ourselves. Otherwise, killing innocent souls is a great sin against Allah," Malam Isa adds. "A great sin."

"But why are these Boko Haram people claiming that they are representing Islam?" Malam Emmanuel asks. "If your Quran teaches all these things, why are they acting differently?"

"They are just ruffians!" Malam Isa replies, his voice raised so loudly that I can hear him from inside the house. "Hooligans, that's what they are, criminals with nothing better to do! They are not reading from the same Quran that I read every day. A true Muslim is one from whose tongue and hands his community is safe. That's what my Quran teaches me."

Somehow, Aisha's goat pepper soup does not taste the same today.

I munch a few pieces of intestine and liver before insisting that I am too full to eat any more.

On our way home, I notice that the bowl in the midst of Malam Isa and his friends has barely been touched.

"Their hostility toward education is because they feel it corrupts," Malam Shettima says. "But that strongly contravenes the teachings of Islam. The very first revelation from Allah to the Prophet Muhammad was the word *Read*. That's what I teach the children in my Islamiya class every Sunday. They must all pursue knowledge."

They are still talking about Boko Haram.

URGENT PRAYER

"GOD IS LEADING ME to call a month of urgent prayer and fasting for the entire church," Pastor Moses says. "We must rise up together and wage spiritual warfare against the forces of darkness behind Boko Haram."

The last time Christ the King Church embarked on an urgent prayer and fasting session was when the rains were late last year.

Going without food and drink from midnight until six p.m. every day for one month was torture, but everyone agreed that it was a necessary spiritual measure for a drastic situation.

Each day of fasting culminated in a five p.m. gathering in the church hall, during which we prayed for an hour. Three days before the fast ended, the rains fell.

I hope that Boko Haram will be annihilated with our prayers.

"We'll begin the week after we return from Prosper's wedding," Pastor Moses adds. "Emmanuel will communicate the date."

Will Success come home with Pastor Moses after the wedding? Will he remember my storybooks? Which of my dresses would I wear when he visited next?

If only I could travel with Mama to attend the wedding. But our church cannot afford to pay the fares of mothers and their children.

BOKO HARAM MEN

Do THEY HAVE HORNS and hooves?
  Are their teeth sharp and pointed?
  Do their nails grow long and curl around their fingers?
  Are their eyes slit and red?
  Do they cook their food or chew it raw?
  Are their voices huffish and gruffish?
  Do they eat human flesh?
  Are their ears long and sharp?

WAITING FOR MAMA

ONCE AGAIN, I STEP out onto the veranda and peer into the horizon. No sign of Mama.

Why is she late returning home from the market?

Again and again, I stretch my neck and peek.

And then her vast raffia basket comes into view!

I sprint forward, not stopping until my head is against her chest and I wrap my arms around her waist.

A KNOCK AT THE DOOR

THE FILM IS ONLY halfway through and we are keen to know what happens after the man slaps his wife for going out with her friends without his permission.

Aisha tears herself away from the screen and goes to answer, while Sarah presses the pause button.

From behind the wooden frame, I hear Malam Isa's voice. It is soft and tender and authoritative. But there is something else in it that I have not heard before.

"Ask your friends to start leaving," he says. "I don't want them to stay too late, so they can reach home before it gets dark."

The something else in his voice is fear.

IN SARAH'S HOUSE

Sometimes, it is impossible for my best friend to keep her once-a-month secret.

On the second or third day, she announces it to the world in screams and yells. She rolls on the floor in her house and wails.

"My stomach! My stomach! My stomach!"

I sit beside her and rub her legs, wishing I could take away the pain, divide it in two and take half in my own body so that she does not have to feel the cramps as intensely.

"Here's some hot tea," her mother says.

"Here are some herbs," her father says.

What can I do to help?

I remember the pink packet hidden deep inside Mama's bag of clothes. Unlike me, Sarah did not bother to save any of hers. I dash back to my house and return bearing the magic pads in my hands.

"Here, Sarah," I say. "You can have these."

That way, she won't have to deal with the pain of the cramps and with the trouble of washing soaked rags at the same time.

ALONE

No singing of familiar tunes or learning new ones. No telling riddles and sharing jokes. No whispering secrets that no other ears will ever hear.

No hands to hold.

Me, alone, walking to school. My best friend is on her period.

There's a rustling in the trees.

"Ahhh!" I scream, and flee as fast as my feet will fly.

But there is no Boko Haram man chasing after me. The raven flaps its wings and takes off.

Even after I walk through my classroom door and sit at my desk, my heart still hammers inside my chest.

SURPRISE

Principal is standing in front of my house. I nearly drop to the ground and die.

What could have brought this revered man here?

After a greeting and a curtsy, I lead him into the living room to see Papa. He insists that I stay with them.

Papa stands from his mat. His eyebrows are furrowed.

He silences his radio.

"You're welcome," Papa says once. "You are welcome," he says twice. "You are welcome," he says again and again.

My school fees were late again this term but Papa eventually paid, for sure, so Principal is not here to collect a debt.

But what else?

"Your daughter has been selected for the Borno State government scholarship program for exceptional children from disadvantaged homes," Principal says. "Anything—anything—she wishes to study right up to master's degree level, the government is willing to pay."

FAME

BY MORNING, EVERY BOY and girl in my school knows.

By afternoon, every father and mother in the village knows.

"Congratulations!"

"You're so lucky!"

"We're so proud of you!"

"I'll miss you when you go," Sarah says. "Make sure you don't forget me."

"I'll never, ever forget you," I say.

I reach for her hand.

Sarah's scores may not have qualified her to sit for the scholarship exam, but she will still be my best friend.

Forever.

I won't abandon someone with whom I've exchanged secrets and clothes and riddles since I was old enough to pronounce words, simply because I am the first child from this village to ever win a government scholarship.

HEARTACHE

By NEXT TERM, I will be in a different world, although on this same planet—in a special boarding school for exceptional girls instead of a village school. One of my sweetest dreams is about to become reality, and yet my heart aches.

It aches for the life I will leave behind.

Laughing with Sarah on our walk to school every morning.

Watching Jacob giggle as he chases lizards around the backyard.

Munching the handful of Buttermint sweets that Papa brings for me whenever he returns from the market after selling his produce. That's how Mama knows the time is right to ask for a new wrapper fabric.

Helping Mama to cook and clean and wash and scrub. How is she going to cope with her Ya Ta gone?

"Don't let that worry you," she says. "Just think how much more help you will be to me when you finish university and get a good job."

Mama is right.

If the vulture satisfies me, then the peacock will pass me by.

WITH A UNIVERSITY DEGREE

I WILL EARN ENOUGH money to ensure that Jacob goes from secondary school to university.

I will have enough to buy a new mattress for Mama to rest her weary back.

And then, if there is still money left over from my salary, I will buy a bicycle for Papa, and an endless supply of batteries for his radio.

I will buy Sarah a new pair of shoes, with heels higher than those of the women in Aisha's DVDs. And as many pink packets of pads as she needs.

THE VOICE ON PAPA'S RADIO

"NIGERIA'S PRESIDENT GOODLUCK JONATHAN has announced the sack of his military high command. No reason was given, but the dismissals come amid growing concern about the military's failure to end the Islamist-led insurgency in northern Nigeria. Mr. Jonathan imposed a state of emergency in three northern Nigerian states in May 2013, giving the military wide-ranging powers to end the insurgency. Several months later, it seems to have had little effect in curbing Boko Haram."

"Thank God that we now have a different set of officers in charge of the army," Papa says. "The other ones must have been doing nothing."

Thank God.

Like Papa, I believe that President Jonathan has chosen new officers who are better prepared and qualified to defeat Boko Haram.

It should now be only a matter of time before the terrorists disappear.

BAD NEWS

PAPA NEVER ALLOWS ANYONE from his family to queue up with the rest of the village when the doctors and nurses from Maiduguri arrive with syringes and stethoscopes in their white van.

"They always bring bad news," he says.

He insists that his mother was healthy until the free health check people appeared, perfectly fine until she received her test results.

Next thing, she was groaning on a mat in the backyard. Then she was traveling to and from the teaching hospital in Maiduguri. Finally, Papa sold our TV set, and still had no money left to pay our fees for an entire year.

Meanwhile, the free health check doctors and nurses had disappeared with their white van. After delivering their bad news, they did not hang around to watch Papa's mother shrivel up in the backyard and die.

"I am not happy about this medical test," Papa says. "I don't want my daughter to do it."

"It is a requirement for every child who gets the scholarship," Principal says. "You need to do it quickly if you're serious about her enrolling at the special school next term. The government needs to see the results of her medical tests before they can issue her admission."

WORRY

Measles
Kwashiorkor
Meningitis
Tetanus
Whooping cough
Tuberculosis
Diarrhea
Polio
HIV/AIDS

From dusk to dawn, my mind runs through the list of diseases I have learned about in science class and from the gory posters on the walls of the general hospital in nearby Gwoza.

Which one of them might keep me from attending the special school?

What might the doctors and nurses find hiding in my body?

Dysentery, malaria, chicken pox—the three major sicknesses I have suffered since birth. Polio passed through our village once and left ten families with cripples, but it did not knock on Papa's door.

I pray that we are as lucky this time. I hope that Papa is wrong about medical tests.

For nothing must come between me and my Borno State government scholarship.

PREGNANCY

THE NURSE AT THE Gwoza General Hospital says that my pregnancy test result will be sent directly to my new school. Thus ends my jittering.

The scholarship board is on the lookout for hidden embryos, not viruses or microbes. I am one hundred percent certain that everything will come out fine.

DANGEROUS COWS

THE MAN IN THE seat in front of me is nodding off. Papa sits beside me listening to his radio. I stare out the window of the bus, just in case something interesting happens on the journey from Gwoza to Damboa, where we board a smaller vehicle that will take us to our village.

Eventually, my diligence pays off, and cows surround our vehicle.

The bus driver weaves the vehicle past the huge horns and robust rumps while the bulky creatures make their way from one side of the road to the other. I marvel at how far Fulani herdsmen are prepared to traverse while grazing their cattle.

When they're in search of greener pastures, Papa says they sometimes roam as far as the southeast of Nigeria, where the Igbo people live, and even to the southwest, where the Yoruba people live.

If only I could sit atop one of the bulls and ride along. What an adventure that would be!

The man in the seat in front of me raises his head and rubs his eyes. He looks lazily out the window. Suddenly, he screams.

"Never drive close to the cows! Never drive close to the cows! The spirit of Boko Haram can enter the cows, so you should always wait for the cows to cross the road!"

Eyes wide with panic, our driver searches around for the best escape route.

"Quick! Quick! Quick!" we all scream as he fiddles with the gears, stamping his foot on the accelerator and flying the bus forward.

Soon, we are away from the cows and safe from danger. Still, my teeth chatter.

"Thank God!" Papa says.

"Thank God," I say.

SUCKING SEEDS

SARAH AND I SLAM our baobab fruits hard on the veranda in her house. After a number of attempts, out tumble the numerous white seeds.

Sitting side by side, we suck each baobab seed clean of its powdery covering, enjoying the sweet and tangy taste in silence. I will miss her when I leave for boarding school.

At the end, my tongue is numb.

"Mine, too," Sarah says. "Maybe that's God's way of warning us that we've eaten too much."

We laugh.

It is time to tell her my news.

"Mama mentioned that Pastor Moses's entire family will be coming here for a thanksgiving service next Sunday," I say. "The new couple plus all his other children. The fasting will start the day after the thanksgiving. That's what Malam Emmanuel told her."

Sarah understands immediately. "Wooooooo!" she sings. "Success is coming, Success is coming, Success is coming. . . ."

"Shhh!" I clap my palm over her mouth.

Yes, my storybooks and my Success.

Just over a week of waiting to go, before I can share my good news with him about the Borno government scholarship, before he will realize that I also will be going on to university like him.

MAMA'S PROMISE

"YA TA, YOU'LL HAVE to take care of the house on your own," Mama says.

A tingle runs down my spine.

"No need to look so worried," she says. "I trust you."

Handling the home in the two days of Mama's absence will be easy, requiring as little effort as tearing a piece of bread. Whatever is inside the chicken, the hawk has been familiar with it for a long time.

I am more worried about Mama and the churchwomen traveling all the way to Jalingo by road. What if their journey is cut short by the appearance of men with bombs and guns in the middle of the highway?

"That won't happen," Mama says. "Jalingo is safe. No Boko Haram in those parts."

She draws me closer, holding my head to her chest.

I inhale her sweet smell of onions and fried oil.

"I'll be back," Mama says. "I promise."

BANG

I STIR THE GROUND corn into the bowl of hot water, careful that the *tuwo's* consistency is light and smooth, the way Papa likes it. He must not feel Mama's absence in any way. He must not notice any discrepancy between her cooking and mine.

I scoop a portion of the steaming dough onto his plate and pat it carefully with a wet spoon. My presentation must be perfect.

I bear the steaming tray of *tuwo* and vegetable stew into the living room, where Papa waits, listening to his radio.

I set it on the stool in front of him when I hear the first bang, cracking like the sound of distant thunder.

"Thank God!" Abraham says. "The rains have come early!"

"Wonderful!" Papa says.

Hooray! I knew it was only a matter of time after Izghe.

Jacob dashes past me, into the backyard. Soon, I hear him singing and dancing with the neighbors' children.

"*Allah ya'kawo ruwa! Allah ya'kawo ruwa!* God bring the rains! God bring the rains! Let the rains come! Let the rains come!"

Early rains deserve a more zealous welcome from us than a visiting local government chairman does. And the children know it.

"*Allah ya'kawo ruwa! Allah ya'kawo ruwa!* God bring the rains! God bring the rains," they shout. "Let the rains come! Let the rains come!"

Bang! Bang! Bang!

More thunder.

"*Allah ya'kawo ruwa! Allah ya'kawo ruwa!* God bring the rains! God bring the rains," they shout. "Let the rains come! Let the rains come!"

Bang! Bang! Bang!

Jacob rushes back into the house and clutches my thighs.

"What is the matter?" I ask.

And then the unmistakable sound of roaring engines not far away. And of screaming children. And of angry guns.

Bang! Bang! Bang!

And of ferocious men.

"*Allahu akbar! Allahu akbar!*" they shout. "Allah is great! Allah is great!"

We scramble outside after the first firebomb lights our thatched roof. Papa reaches for his machete leaning against the wall in the veranda. The man on the motorbike fires his gun.

Bang!

No time for me to think or feel as Papa drops to the floor. The men on motorbikes are everywhere, firing their weapons in the air.

Men, women, boys, and girls scatter out of their homes and toward the hills.

Boko Haram is in our village.

. . . And when all were in to the very last,
The door in the mountain-side shut fast.
Did I say, all? No! One was lame,
And could not dance the whole of the way;
And in after years, if you would blame
His sadness, he was used to say,—
"It's dull in our town since my playmates left!
I can't forget that I'm bereft . . ."

—Robert Browning, "The Pied Piper of Hamelin"

GONE

IT IS DIFFICULT TO say for how long I have been traveling in the back of this dusty truck, but it is long enough for my well of tears to finally run dry. As the vehicle trundles deeper and deeper into the dark forest, the ugly truth finally sinks into my head.

Papa and his repertoire of tales, stories of his childhood, of ghosts and witches, of hyenas and hares that could speak fluent Hausa like the rest of us.

Abraham and his plan to find a good girl to marry by next year, if the harvest was good, and Elijah and Caleb and Isaac.

Principal and all the knowledge from his dozens of books, his fluid English and his white-man ways.

Malam Zwindila and his intolerance of anything but the correct answer, his joy at being a groom and a new father.

Malam Isa and his love for Aisha, his prayers to Allah five times a day.

All dead, slaughtered, gone forever, never to materialize again.

And Jacob, my dear baby brother, inside a different dusty truck, on our journey into the unknown.

REASONS TO THANK GOD

I THANK GOD THAT I am not alone. Papa and Mama and my brothers may not be here with me, but there are dozens of other girls packed into the truck, with Sarah at my right and Aisha at my front.

I thank God that I am a girl. Girls fry the *kosai* and *massa*, then wait for the boys to have their fill before they eat what is left in the pan. Girls shred their fingers sore on the sharp stones and broken glass forgotten by the boys in their trouser pockets before they tossed them onto the pile of weekly laundry. But it was the boys and men that got called to one side of the building when the Boko Haram men gathered all the villagers they could capture and led us to the mosque, those who were not fast enough to run toward the hills and hide.

It was the boys and men who were instructed to step outside.

It was the boys and men who glanced backward and told their mothers, sisters, and wives not to be afraid.

It was the boys who were lying in shallow puddles of red, while the girls and women and toddlers were marched into trucks, leaving only the elderly behind.

I thank God that I still have one brother left, that Jacob and the other children are following behind in another truck.

Peter's brothers also have a lot to thank God for. They were the only male captives who did not run away but who did not get slaughtered by the Boko Haram men. Peter's brothers may have led a hard life as a result of having one leg almost three times shorter than the other because of polio, but their disability is the reason why the Boko Haram men asked them to leave the mosque and limp back home in peace.

I thank God that Pastor Moses fixed Prosper's wedding this weekend.

I thank God that Papa gave Mama the permission to travel to Jalingo with Sarah's mother and the other women.

I thank God that Success was not visiting his parents this weekend. I thank God that he is most likely still alive.

FIRST STEP

THE JOURNEY THAT BEGAN in the mild light of the moon ends in the dim light of late noon. Only a traveler who has come and gone along the same route a billion times could possibly recognize the way home.

The back of the truck falls open and it is my turn to jump off. The truck with Jacob and the other children disappears farther into the forest. What are they going to do with my baby brother?

I let go of Sarah's hand and leap.

My first step in the Sambisa forest.

SLAVES

"You belong to Boko Haram," the Leader says. "You are now our slaves."

His voice is as calm as glass. His face is as blank as a stone. His arm is drawn up to his chest with the long, black barrel in his hands pointing straight at us, a finger resting on the trigger.

Scores of men stand a reverent two or three paces behind him. They also are wielding guns and wearing army camouflage uniforms with black boots and trousers that stop short of their ankles.

"Don't try to run away," he says. "If you do, the land mines will blow you to pieces."

NEW MASTERS

DANLADI ONCE TOLD US that the Sambisa used to be home to monkeys and antelopes, lions and elephants, all sorts of birds—including ostriches that laid eggs as large as a soursop.

"Tweet-tweet, tu-whoo, hee-haw, dook-dook, everywhere you go in the Sambisa," he said.

The white people who came to see the animals could not venture too deep inside the forest. Only the most skilled hunters, such as his grandfather, dared enter certain parts of the Sambisa where the skin of human beings would be pierced by thorns. The animals' thick skins made them immune to the poisonous prickles.

Danladi told us his father said it did not matter that the Sambisa forest was so vast, stretching to so many states. "It belongs to Borno," he said.

After all, the Sambisa village from where the forest got its name was not too far away from Gwoza, a few kilometers from our own village.

"It belongs to us," he insisted. "The Sambisa belongs to the people of Borno."

Not anymore.

Boko Haram is its new master.

MAD MAN

"WE DO NOT INTEND to harm you," the Leader says. "We only want to make you good Muslim women."

Gripping each other's fingers tight, Sarah and I shift to his left-hand side with the other Christian women and girls, while Aisha stands on the right with the Muslims.

Like many of those in her group, the entire upper part of Aisha's body is hidden inside a hijab; yet the Boko Haram men do not judge by sight alone. Three armed men stomp from one girl to the other, commanding each to recite her full name and a snippet of the Quran.

With her eyes cast down upon her bulging belly, Aisha rattles off a lengthy text of the Muslim holy book in Arabic. Her rendition is fluent, as if she were reading from a slate in the sand at her bare feet.

Malam Isa would have been proud.

Now certain that Aisha and the rest are indeed followers of Islam, some Boko Haram men lead them away. Would they be allowed to go home, to whatever is left of their houses and families?

The women and girls disappear toward the cluster of tarpaulin tents visible between the coarse trunks and scattered shrubs. The Leader grips the butt of his gun with his right hand; his left clutches the barrel.

"Are you people ready to convert to Islam?" he asks.

Silence.

Except for the thumping of my heart against my chest—which must be loud enough to wake a sleeping child—no one makes a sound.

"Are you ready to become Muslims?" he asks again.

I clutch Sarah's fingers tighter. She squeezes my hand.

"Those of you who want to become Muslims should move to the right," he says.

He relaxes his hold on the gun and lets it dangle by a shoulder strap toward the ground.

My heart stops galloping against my chest. I take a deep breath and relax my hold on Sarah.

I have an idea what is coming next.

Pastor Moses concluded some sermons in Christ the King Church by asking if anyone sitting in the congregation wanted to give their life to Jesus. He then asked them to rise to their feet.

Sometimes, one person stood up. Other times, two or three. There was a particular Sunday morning last December when about five or six stood. These people who wanted to become Christians were then told to repeat a prayer after Pastor Moses, and then he welcomed them to the family of Jesus.

The Leader most likely wants the new converts to say a prayer after him.

But I am happy with being a Christian, never mind that I

often wished that Pastor Moses's Sunday sermon did not go on till eternity, and that I sometimes exchanged cheeky whispers with Sarah about the woman's mustache whenever Magdalene's mother stood on stage to sing.

I remain standing on the left-hand side of the Leader. So do Sarah and dozens of other women and girls. Only seven or eight from our group shuffle slowly toward the right, their heads drooping.

I wonder if Pastor Moses might be ashamed to see his committed members openly abandoning the Christian faith. I wonder if he might understand.

The Leader catches the eye of one of the men at the back and nods his head ever so slightly. The man hurries off into the forest, the same direction as the Muslim girls.

Through the stems and shrubs, the Boko Haram man hurries back. In his right hand, he waves a curved knife with a pointed blade that reflects the rays from the sun. In his left hand, he drags an elderly man dressed in a green Nigerian army uniform, whose wrists and ankles are bound with rope.

"You do not want to convert to Islam?" the Leader says.

As quick as lightning, the deed is done. I clap my palms over my eyes and scream.

"We will kill all of you the same way if you refuse to convert," the Leader says.

We drop to our knees and beg.

"No, please! Please, don't kill us!"

In the past twenty-four hours, I have seen more blood and

bodies to feed my nightmares for the next two thousand years. I have wished that death had taken me along with Papa and my brothers. But the sight of that soldier's gray head resting a few inches from his bare feet, with the eyes and mouth frozen open, gives me a fresh desire to preserve my life.

"I want to be a Muslim!" I cry.

"Yes, I will convert!" Sarah wails.

"I will convert!" others scream.

Only Magdalene is left standing on the left-hand side, straight as a steeple.

Eyes closed. Hands raised toward heaven.

She opens her mouth and sings. "Jesus loves me, this I know / For the Bible tells me so / Little ones to Him belong—"

For the first time, the Leader loses his aura of control. Back when he gathered us in the village mosque, he was guffawing like a hyena, mocking the fathers for allowing their daughters to waste Allah's time by going to school instead of getting married, and assuring them that he would soon right that wrong.

This time, he is as livid as a wasp. The mad man hiding inside him shines darkly through his swollen eyeballs.

I wish I were bold enough to open my mouth and beg Magdalene to stop. Slaughtering innocent boys and decapitating elderly men is certainly not the Islam that I have known and seen; I wish Magdalene would stop being stubborn and convert along with us.

The Leader stomps over and slams his fist into Magdalene's mouth. "Shut up!" he barks.

Magdalene crumples. She continues to sing.

"They are weak . . . but He is . . . strong / Yes, Jesus . . . loves me / Yes . . ."

He raises his gun and cocks it. He changes his mind and lets the gun dangle at his side.

". . . Jesus . . . loves me—"

He stretches out his hand.

"Al-Bakura, give it to me!"

The man who dragged in and slaughtered the soldier hands him the murder weapon.

I wrap my arms around Sarah. She folds her arms around me and buries her head in my neck. I shut my eyes and ears tight.

DARKNESS

Armed men are surrounding us, guards who have promised to deal mercilessly with anyone who attempts to escape. Yet, I still have space to accommodate another terror, to fret about the unseen creatures.

Ruffling the tree branches above.

Rustling the carpet of leaves underneath.

Ripping the air with their squalls.

Still stored in my mind are Danladi's tales of hissing rattlesnakes and whopping crustaceans crawling about in the Sambisa forest, where the grass can be as high as a teacher's table.

I close my eyes and pray that all the animals out scouring for their meals prefer the taste of leaves or rodents to that of unarmed girls.

I pray that Jacob is asleep and not afraid.

I IMAGINE MAMA

RETURNING FROM JALINGO TO find that all the houses are carcasses, charred blocks and blackened metal.

Passing building after building in horror, wondering how many lightning bolts could have struck the village.

Footsteps quicken along the dirt road to our house. Soon, she breaks into a sprint.

Lips move in emergency prayers, urgent requests for the disaster to have missed her home.

Dinky traveling bag falls to the ground as the tragedy stares her in the face, her husband lying limp in the front yard and the rest of her family gone.

The first scream that comes rolling out from deep inside her intestines, a sound that travels all the way across the village.

Eyes expand in shock as the surviving villagers relay their version of events, those lucky to have fled to the hills.

Breaking away from the thin crowd and rushing off to the village mosque in search of her sons, not believing everything she has been told. Her scarf comes loose from her head. The patterned cloth drops to the floor. Her shoes slip off her feet. She does not care.

Falling over her sons and rattling their bodies to wake them up.

Rushing toward the Sambisa forest, hoping to find Jacob and me.

Falling on her face amid the thorns and shrubs, realizing that it is nothing but a futile attempt.

Begging God to bring her Ya Ta home.

Weeping her eyes out of their sockets. For days on end, no word from heaven or earth would be sufficient to make her stop.

If only I were there to remind Mama to always remain thankful, no matter in what situation she finds herself.

If only she were here to hold me tight, assure me that there is a reason for everything.

SURPRISED

THE TEARS HAVE NOT yet finished. There are still more left inside my eyes.

ꟾNSIDE THE SAMBISA

THERE ARE BATTALIONS OF Boko Haram men everywhere, like ants in an anthill. Going, coming, sitting, standing, walking, chatting, praying, preaching, teaching, training.

Their black flag, imprinted with white Arabic letters above and within a white circle, hangs almost as high as the tallest tree.

Scores of vans and trucks and hundreds of motorbikes are parked in the bowels of the forest. Electricity generators churn. Electrical equipment buzzes. Tarpaulin tents are sprawled from east to west.

Strolling in and out of the shelters are not only Boko Haram men, but dozens of women and children as well. The women stare stealthily at us new arrivals from time to time, as if they are afraid to be caught looking.

But, no matter how hard we may stare back, there is little of them to see.

Their entire bodies are hidden inside mauve niqabs, which allow me to see only their hands and flashes of their eyes.

MOURNING

So MANY WOMEN AND girls gathered in one place, yet hardly any laughing or chitchat.

No new skirt or shoe to admire, no trader or vendor with whom to haggle.

We are like dead people mourning other people who are dead. We are like ghosts stuck between the land of humans and the land of spirits.

All of us except the Boko Haram men, who sometimes laugh and yak all through the night. And Al-Bakura, who loudly recalls in grisly detail how they captured our village.

"I wish I'd had my video camera with me," he says. "You should have seen the way all of you were scurrying like rats."

DAGGER

THE MAD MAN ENTERS a Hilux van followed by other vans filled with Boko Haram men. Their convoy leaves a fog of dust behind.

Unfortunately, they did not take Al-Bakura along.

"If I catch any girl trying to escape, I'm going to slice off her head," he says, a dagger dangling from his right hand.

AL-BAKURA

HE LEAPS AFTER ME with a dagger gleaming in his right hand.

"I am going to slice off your head!" he howls.

Faster and faster, I flee, the sound of his feet getting closer by the second.

Almost out of breath, I notice a dense hedge up ahead. It becomes my goal.

I tuck my body beneath it and lie stationary until he springs past, still howling fearsome threats about what he will do to my head. Soon, his voice disappears. My breathing gradually returns to normal.

Suddenly, out of the darkness, a hand grabs my hair.

"Did you really think you could outrun me?" he asks.

I scream.

And wake up from my nightmare.

ANOTHER LEADER

HER FINGERS ARE DECKED in colorful rings. Her wrist is draped with shiny bangles. Her eyes are painted black and gold.

"I am Amira," she says, adding that her husband is an amir, a commander. "My husband is one of Allah's greatest fighters."

She gives me a mauve hijab and teaches me how to adjust it over my face, so that my ears are tucked neatly inside. I have watched Aisha do this dozens of times before but never imagined I might have to learn it myself.

Within a short while, my armpits are dripping wet. The heat inside makes me want to scream.

"Aisha, I can't believe that you've dressed like this almost all your life," Sarah says.

"It's not so bad," Aisha replies. "Once you get used to it, you'll be fine."

"I don't want to get used to it," I say.

COMFORT

HOLDING HANDS WITH OUR fingers intertwined tight.

Lying side by side with her breath cooling my neck.

Resting my head on her shoulder with her arm around my waist.

My best friend and I, afraid but not alone, deep inside the Sambisa forest.

THE VOICE ON PAPA'S RADIO

WOULD IT TELL PEOPLE in other parts of the world what had happened to us?

Would it announce the exact number of people in our village slain with Papa and my brothers?

Would they hear and come looking for us deep inside the Sambisa, or would they assume that all the girls simply disappeared by charm or magic?

In a way, Mama's prediction came to pass. Papa and his radio left this world together.

I wonder for how long it continued talking before the flames silenced it forever.

FOOD

"YOU HAD BETTER EAT your food, because you are going to be spending a long time with us," Amira says.

I shudder.

We sit in groups of about fifteen to twenty around wide enamel basins set on the floor. Amira selects a girl from each group to fetch one of the pails filled with a soggy, steaming substance and pours it into the basin.

The hunger in my belly burns like a razor cut, but it is impossible to eat. The food looks like white vomit.

"There is no way I can put this in my mouth," I mumble.

"Never. I would rather starve to death," Sarah murmurs.

Like many other girls in our group, Sarah and I turn our faces away from the steaming corn porridge. At least no one is likely to slash our necks for refusing to eat.

But Aisha, sitting two groups away from us, dips into the basin for the third or fourth time. She plunges her hand into her mouth and sucks each finger swiftly, as if she is in a hurry to be done feeding so that she can store her fingers up in the roof to dry.

"Maybe the food is not as bad as it looks," I say.

Sarah agrees to join me in giving it a try.

I stretch my hand toward the basin, but I pull back to let

her go first. She scoops some porridge and waits while I scoop mine.

Together, we open our mouths wide and place the yucky blob on our tongues.

"Pwuuuuuuuua!"

"God forbid!"

It tastes like minced raffia mat!

The corn must have been infested with weevils. Or may have been cooked along with the chaff instead of sieved after grinding. Whatever the case, I have been eating ground corn, as *tuwo* or *pap* or *massa*, all my life, and it has never tasted this revolting before.

As Sarah and I look around for a free space on the ground on which to toss the spat-out food in our palms, it occurs to me: Aisha may be the one scooping the vile food, but it is the baby in her belly doing the eating.

I pray our next meal will be better.

MAGDALENE'S SONG

INSECTS SIP BLOOD FROM all over my arms and feet, but I have run out of strength to keep slapping them away and scratching at their stings.

Sounds of sniffing and sniffling seep into the air everywhere around me, girls with tears left to shed.

The emotions sit in my heart like a brick at the bottom of the lake. Nothing left with which to wash away my pain and dilute my grief.

I cannot sleep. I cannot imagine how tomorrow will be. I cannot endure the thought of another day inside the Sambisa forest.

Another day with Magdalene's song replaying in my mind.

Another day wondering where the truck has taken Jacob, my one and only brother.

RIJALE

I AM STILL NOT sure whether all those legends about the Boko Haram men are true, but there are some facts I know.

Al-Bakura tells us that Boko Haram is doing the work of God. "May Allah continue to give us the courage to change the world," he says. How could they possibly imagine that any god could be pleased with what they do?

They refer to one another as *rijale*, strong men, brave fighters. "Each one of us has the strength of ten men," Al-Bakura says.

They speak different languages. Some speak Hausa, some Kanuri, some Arabic. And one or two other languages that are strange to my ears.

The Boko Haram men follow us everywhere we go, like buttocks on our backsides. When we go to fetch water from the truck that trundles in once every week or two with a full tank, they accompany us. When we go into the nearby bush to toilet, they hover nearby. When we study the Quran, they stand around, listening as we recite passage after passage.

Some of the guards appear to be about the same age as the boys in my class at school, with smooth chins and voices that switch pitch in between sentences.

The younger Boko Haram men are more garrulous than

the older ones. Like women selling onions and tomatoes in the market, their mouths move nonstop with the latest irrelevant information. "It is boring standing around all day, guarding women. I prefer to go out and fight jihad!" they say, keen to join the so-called holy war against infidels.

Some Boko Haram men are tall, with skin as dark as the bottom of a pot. Some are light skinned, with silky, curly hair—like those of people from across the border in the neighboring Republic of Chad. Some have thick, black hair; some have long hair, which they plait into braids. Some wear turbans on their heads.

Al-Bakura has bowlegs and skinny arms, and an oblong head around which he wraps a brown checked cloth. His skin is as black as his long beard.

The one thing they all have in common—tall, short, light, or dark—is the smell of their bodies.

Simply by inhaling two sniffs when he came into the house, I could always tell when Jacob had been playing with Malam Aliyu's goats and sheep instead of sitting on the veranda practicing his alphabets. I could smell whenever a rat was grooming its whiskers behind the sack of millet in Mama's kitchen.

I can smell when Al-Bakura approaches, and when he has been joined by one or two of his cohorts. I can smell when he is creeping into our sleeping area in the middle of the night. I can smell him on the women who return early in the morning with marks on their skin.

It is not the same kind of whiff that Papa and my brothers

gave off whenever they returned from a day of planting seeds or uprooting weeds. It is also not the same smell as Abraham after he had been playing football with Muhammadu and Hussein, who lived down the road.

The Boko Haram men give off a feral scent, as if they had been born and bred in the wild. They smell like human beasts.

INCOMPLETE WOMAN

THE WOMEN IN NIQABS are the Boko Haram wives. Some have fresh eyes; some have crow's-feet. Some have silky hands; some have lizard skin. The full veil reveals little of their features. Although only glimpses of their faces show, their voices do a good job of relating exactly how they feel.

The abuse begins as soon as they see us, whenever we walk past them on our way to the water truck.

"Slaves!"

"Infidels!"

"Dirt!"

On and on the venom flows. The wives never get tired.

Of all the wives, Amira seems to be one of the few who is not complete: childless, never a baby straddling her waist or strapped to her back.

LIFE OF A SLAVE

FETCH WATER FROM THE truck and wash the bloodied shirts of the Boko Haram men who have returned from fighting jihad.

Offload clothes and gadgets and armory from the trucks and vans. If there are sacks of grain among the newly arrived loot, take them to Amira in the cooking area.

Cook for Amira and some of the other Boko Haram wives, for the Boko Haram men who have no wives yet, and for the boys who guard the compound.

Cook for ourselves. When the sack of grain is running low, take turns to go into the forest and harvest green vegetables to add to the meal.

Fetch water from the truck, and wash the pots and basins.

Stay confined to our section of the camp, among tree roots and stems, no straying toward the tarpaulin tents.

Lie on the bare ground under the sky and thank God that Jacob and the other children were wrong, that the rains are yet to arrive.

MAYBE

MAYBE THE HEARTS WERE still beating inside some of the men and boys, never mind that they were lying in a pool of blood outside the mosque.

Maybe someone who made it safely up the hills returned in the nick of time and rushed the lucky survivors to the hospital.

Maybe Abraham, Elijah, Caleb, and Isaac are still alive.

Maybe a skillful looter gathered all our clothes and belongings before the fire traveled from our roof to our walls and floors.

Maybe Papa's radio is still alive and well, perched between the ear and shoulder of a Boko Haram man inside the Sambisa.

TANTALIZER

A TRAY OF STEAMING *kosai* is lowered to the earth in front of me. I lean forward and swallow some whiffs of the tantalizing aroma, my nostrils allowing my tongue a taste of things to come. Saliva fills my mouth.

Just as I reach out to grab one of the balls, a charred hand appears out of nowhere and snatches the tray out of sight.

I jolt awake, panting.

A PROPOSAL

BOILED CORN, BOILED BEEF, boiled rice. But not a bite for our mouths. With great effort, I restrain myself from leaping forward and plunging into the contents of her plate.

"If you marry a Boko Haram commander, your life will be much better," Amira says with a mouthful. "You will have as much food as you want."

Never.

I would rather slave till my fingers peeled or till my back snapped in two. I would rather starve till my tongue withered inside my mouth.

"You remember that film we watched where the bride and groom danced with all the bridesmaids in a circle?" Sarah asks.

I nod.

But all that seems so long ago, in a world that has since disappeared.

MALAM ADAMU

HE TEACHES US QURANIC classes.

He shows us in which direction to bow and kneel, so that we face the holy city of Mecca while praying to Allah.

He makes sure that we pray at dawn, before sunrise; at midday, after the sun passes its highest; in the late part of the afternoon; just after sunset; between sunset and midnight.

He shows us how to perform ablution, washing our hands, mouth, nose, face, arms, head, and ears—making us clean enough to talk to Allah.

He slaps the head of anyone who does not carry out the ritual washing correctly, calling her a daughter of an infidel.

He lands his koboko on anyone still sleeping when it is time for morning prayers.

He assigns us passages of the Quran to learn.

He makes us stand one after the other and recite what we have memorized.

He ensures that our free time is spent listening to sermons.

He tiptoes into our sleeping area after dark, noiseless as a shadow, taps a woman or two, and beckons her to follow him out quietly.

THE WORST STUDENT

INSIDE A POT OF soup, the horse is a less valuable animal than the hen. Inside Malam Adamu's classroom, all the mathematical formulas and the conjugated verbs I know are useless.

In this new school, I am the worst student.

Hardly a day goes by without a lashing of the koboko. My brain seems to have turned to sawdust.

No matter how hard I try, it is difficult to push away thoughts of my Borno State government scholarship and concentrate in a school where the teacher tells me that reading books is a sin against Allah, that Western education is haram, taboo.

LIAR

AL-BAKURA TELLS US THAT Boko Haram is taking over the world.

He tells us that there is no other type of government apart from Sharia.

He tells us that democracy means government of Allah, for Allah, and by Allah.

He tells us that we are not a part of Nigeria.

He tells us that Islam is the only true religion.

He tells us that the Quran is the only book worth reading.

He tells us that our fathers and brothers deserved to die because they were infidels who did not believe in Allah.

MY NAME

I DO NOT WANT a name different from what Papa and Mama called me. But changing my name to an Islamic one is the next step in becoming a good Muslim woman, and I dare not argue with Malam Adamu.

"You shall be called Salamatu," he says.

Sarah's new name is Zainab.

Remembering Pastor Moses's sermon about the importance of names, I am worried.

"Aisha, what does 'Salamatu' mean?" I ask.

"Salamatu means 'safety,'" she replies. "It's Arabic."

Safety from guns and knives. Safety from nighttime predators, human and nonhuman.

I hope that this new name is a good omen, a sign of what lies ahead for me.

LASHING

AL-BAKURA SLAMS THE KOBOKO against the back of my leg. Once, twice, thrice.

"Argh!"

"What is her name?"

"Her name is Zainab."

"What is her name?"

"Zainab!"

"What is her name?"

"Argh! Zainab!"

"I never want to hear you calling her Sarah again."

SITTING ON A ROCK

ZAINAB PLAITS MY THICK strands into straight cornrows, the ends scratching the back of my head.

I plait Zainab's soft strands into thick cornrows, the ends drooping over the back of her neck, the stench striking my nose.

PRAYER

NIGHT AFTER NIGHT, I pray that it will not be my turn. I pray that Al-Bakura and Malam Adamu will choose someone else.

Night after night, my shameful heart rejoices as they tiptoe past me and on to someone else.

"Thank God," I mutter.

Maybe I am not beautiful enough. Maybe my waist is not broad enough. Maybe my breasts are not big enough.

But then, they have not taken Zainab away either.

Whatever the case, I am grateful.

I am untouched. I am safe.

I am Salamatu.

ESCAPE

A PARTICULARLY VIGOROUS FLAPPING of wings interrupts my hard efforts at sleep. I catch sight of an indistinguishable bird as it takes off from a treetop, soaring higher and higher into the sky.

If only an angel would appear up there with the stars. If only it would fly down from the clouds. I would mount its wings and fly far, far away from the Sambisa forest and home to Mama.

I jolt at a whisper.

Zainab's voice.

"What did you say?"

Slowly, she repeats herself.

"Magdalene is lucky," she says. "Magdalene is in a better place. She made the better choice."

TORMENT

THESE DAYS, MY NIGHTMARES feature neither bullets nor bombs. No demons hunt me. No mad men threaten me. Not even Al-Bakura appears.

Instead, I am tormented by fried chicken and roasted corn and *acha* and *kosai* and *massa*.

Night after night, a different food takes its turn to torture me while I sleep.

TREE OF DEATH

INTO THE FOREST, ZAINAB and I go in search of vegetables for today's meal.

Our feet crush through the carpet of soft soil and dry leaves beyond the parked trucks. Our eyes scan the short trees and shrubs for a familiar plant that will not bring death into the cooking pot.

This is the farthest we have ever been away from the camp.

We crouch beneath branches. We push aside thorns. Al-Bakura sits on the ground and rests his gun on his lap. He digs his hand into his crotch.

From inside his underwear, he pulls out a mobile phone and turns on the music.

"Ehn doro bucci / Don doro bucci / Doro Jazzy / Ehn doro boss . . ."

Isaac's favorite song. Whenever it was playing on Papa's radio, my brother stopped whatever he was doing and dipped his two hands into his pockets like a rich man, bobbing his head from side to side to the rhythm.

He used to say that he would one day become as rich as Don Jazzy, the singer, and then get married to Tiwa Savage. But I knew that he was only joking. Papa would never allow him to marry a woman who was not Hausa, not even if she was a famous musician.

I grab Zainab's arm.

"Look!"

Her eyes, terrified, follow my finger.

Her eyes twinkle like a candle flame sprinkled with salt.

"Hallelujah!"

"Thank God!"

A baobab tree!

Zainab and I hurry toward the tree of life, knowing that today's corn meal will be the most delicious of our lives. And if the ground underneath is free of sharp stones, maybe she will crouch while I stand to pluck some of its fruits. My tongue gets set for a trip to heaven.

Soon, we notice the smell. The nearer we go, the stronger the stench. Like the smell of a rat that has succumbed to Mama's Superkill Action–laced crayfish. Like the smell of the cow entrails from Divine's naming ceremony.

"What is that smell?" I ask.

Zainab covers her nose with her hijab. Her response is muffled in the mauve cloth.

And then I see it.

A vast hole beneath the baobab tree. A cloud of flies swimming above.

I retch.

I now know what became of the elderly soldier, Magdalene, and the girl who slumped during Quranic class.

FERTILIZER

SITTING IN QURANIC CLASS and listening to Malam Adamu teach us how to become good Muslim women, my mind wanders to Papa's bags of fertilizer.

Every farming season for the past few years, Papa and every other farmer in our village received a text message from the government on his mobile phone letting him know that the subsidized fertilizer was ready for collection.

Together, all the farmers traveled by bus to the local government office, where they were each given two bags at a third of the market price.

What will the government do with Papa's share this year? Will the officials notice that he is absent? How many farmers from our village will also not be present to collect their fertilizer?

TIRED

"I AM TIRED OF all these stupid prayers!" Zainab groans.

"Me too. But you'll get into trouble if you don't go," I say.

Aisha stands quietly, saying nothing.

"I don't care anymore," she says. "Let Al-Bakura kill me if he likes. I'm tired."

"Zainab, please, don't do anything stupid," I say.

"You can tell him that you're on your period," Aisha says.

Malam Adamu taught us that, while menstruating, we are unfit to talk to Allah.

Unless Allah reveals it to him, he will have no way of knowing that Zainab has told him a lie.

BITE OFF HIS EARS

EVENTUALLY, I DETECT WHAT is happening. I notice something I had not before.

The Boko Haram men who come into our sleeping area at night are not interested in the girls. They are only after the women.

All those they ask to come along with them in the middle of the night are years older than Zainab and me.

"Maybe we can escape before we are old enough to go with them," I say.

"I will kill anyone who tries to touch me," Zainab says. "I will bite off his ears."

AISHA'S TURN

TONIGHT, IT IS AISHA'S turn to go with Al-Bakura. Her pregnancy probably makes them think that she is a woman.

"No! No! Please! Please!" Aisha screams. "I am a married woman! I am expecting a child!"

The rest of us lie silent, pretending that our ears are dead.

If only I could do something to help. If only I could inform Al-Bakura that he is making a mistake, that Aisha is not really a woman, that she is the same age as Zainab and me.

But no matter how much the tortoise may wish to fight, he has no fingers.

Aisha's wailing gets louder and louder. Al-Bakura does not take her revolt lightly. A dull sound. A muffled cry. The end of Aisha's resistance.

"Shut up or I will kill you," he says.

THIS IS NOT ISLAM

AISHA RETURNS JUST BEFORE dawn with her hijab askew. Zainab and I sit up beside her, gripping her shoulders and patting her head.

"This is not Islam," she says once. "This is not Islam," she says again. "This is not Islam," she says over and over again.

NOTHING TO DO WITH ISLAM

I HAVE BEEN THINKING the same thing myself. And not just because I heard Malam Isa and Malam Shettima say as much during their goat-meat-pepper-soup argument. And not because I have closely watched Malam Isa and Aisha practice their religion.

I have been reflecting on the issue since we began Quranic classes, and the contradictions seem to increase by the day.

Could Islam, whose name Malam Adamu teaches us stands for peace and submission to God, encourage its adherents to work for the death and destruction of human beings?

Could the same Allah who asked his followers to give alms to beggars with jiggers in their feet also ask them to slaughter unarmed boys?

Every sura in the Quran that Malam Adamu reads out to us begins with "Bismillah." Malam Adamu says that, similarly, any action by humans must start the same way. But how can you start your deeds with "In the name of God, the Most Gracious, the Most Merciful," and yet raze villages and destroy homes?

What was gracious about taking girls away in the middle of the night? What was merciful about stabbing a girl who was singing about Jesus's love for her?

Malam Isa and Malam Shettima were right. Boko Haram has nothing to do with changing the world. Boko Haram has nothing to do with Allah.

Boko Haram has nothing to do with Islam.

EDUCATION

THE BOKO HARAM MEN claim that Western education is taboo. They say it is haram for women to go to school.

If they hated Western education so much, why did they bother with guns and trucks, which you could learn how to make only by going to school?

Why did they drive Hilux vans and motorbikes, which could only have been invented with the knowledge of science and technology?

MY DEFINITION OF HARAM

STEALING CHILDREN FROM THEIR papa and mama.

Hitting a pregnant woman.

Tiptoeing into a woman's sleeping area at midnight and commanding her to follow you out.

OPEN SECRET

ONCE AGAIN, THE CRAMPS expose Zainab's secret to the world.

Just like that, Allah reveals to Al-Bakura that she had faked her period the last time.

He refuses to swallow her insistence that a strange occurrence in her body has led to two cycles so close in time.

I shut my eyes and ears tight, but the sound of the koboko landing still pierces through.

Twenty-five lashes on her back.

MALAM ISA

ALL THE BEGGARS IN our village hobbled to his front door on Friday afternoons like soldier ants on a sugar trail.

When they saw him returning from the mosque, they stretched out their cracked palms and cried, *"Allah ya ba mu alheri! Allah ya ba mu alheri!"* Then they muttered prayers for Allah to continue to make him strong and his farms to produce great harvest.

Whenever Zainab and I spent extended periods with Aisha during the holidays, I saw Malam Isa dip into the pocket of his caftan and hand out red and green naira notes to each of the beggars.

There was no instance when he hissed or frowned or shooed them away like flies hovering over his *tuwo shinkafi* lunch, not even when the rains were late last year and his groundnut, onions, and tomato crops did not yield as bountifully.

He was determined to obey the Quran's instruction to give alms especially after Friday prayers at the mosque. Malam Isa was a good Muslim man, in happy times or bad.

Allah would certainly not be happy to have watched this good man be butchered like a Christmas chicken.

And here is Malam Adamu, one of those responsible for Malam Isa's death, teaching us in Quranic class how to become good Muslim women.

TALES BY MOONLIGHT

"WE ATTACKED GIWA BARRACKS in Maiduguri and freed more than seven hundred of our brave fighters who were arrested by the Nigerian military," Al-Bakura says. "Gwoza, Mafa, Dikwa, Banki, Baga, Monguno . . . all these towns and many others are now part of our caliphate. Boko Haram is in control and everyone there now lives under Sharia law."

Above in the sky, the full moon gleams, the only visible beauty in this dark and frightening world.

Al-Bakura's tales by moonlight are definitely not the same as Papa's. His bring sorrow instead of laughter and learning.

DEATH

No matter how many koboko strikes Al-Bakura lands on her, Jamila does not open her eyes.

Throughout yesterday, she stooped and spat, her entire body quaking with cough. But no slave in the Sambisa is entitled to medicine.

"When you get married, things will change," Amira says.

BATTLE

As SOON AS THE cooked meal is poured into the basin, the battle begins. No time to waste. Speed is key.

I shift forward and elbow a hand in my path. I dip into the basin and tackle some fingers that interfere with mine. I fill my palm with as much fluid as it will contain, then toss back my head and lap up the watery cornmeal. I dive in for another round.

I must act fast, plunge in and out as many times as possible before Aisha lifts the basin over her head and licks the last drops clinging to the enamel.

In the twinkling of an eye, mealtime is over.

And yet, I am still hungry.

After the battle is fought and won, my stomach continues to burn, as if a bicycle with square wheels is riding around inside.

To think that there was a time when I sat on the veranda waiting for Mama, imagining that I knew the true meaning of hunger.

ONE OF A KIND

THE HUNGER IN THE Sambisa forest is different from the kind that stood with me on the veranda while I eagerly awaited Mama's return from the market.

This hunger is unique.

It is the kind of hunger that is not satisfied with staying inside your stomach to sizzle your intestines. Soon, it migrates to your head and makes you feel as if you are dangling on the brink of a cliff off which you might fall any moment, stopping along the way to siphon all the strength from your muscles and bones. Henceforth, a snail may beat you in a race.

It is the kind of hunger that makes you think no other thought but the next meal. Each time the wind flaps the plastic sheets that provide some privacy for the area where you squat into a hole in the ground to obey nature's demands, you sit up, imagining that someone might be approaching with a bucket of food. Each time a guard fiddles with the barrel of his gun while describing his most recent jihad exploit to another guard who is merely a new conscript, you stretch your neck, hoping that an enamel basin of food has indeed been set on the floor.

It is the kind of hunger that takes over your body and soul, forcing your eyelids shut and stealing your attention from

Malam Adamu's Quranic lessons. The longer he speaks, the faster the suras go in my ear and make a U-turn right out of the same ear. When we pray to Allah, I summon enough strength to beg Him to send me some food. What I want most in the world is a hefty meal, after which I will put my head down on anything, hard or soft, and snooze until the world comes to a happy end.

It is the kind of hunger that follows you right into your sleep. It teases you in your nightmares and taunts your appetite with impossible meals. Sometimes, the aroma from my dream lingers after I wake, wetting my tongue with a stream of sour saliva.

It is the kind of hunger that bars you from caring about anyone else. Your belly is your only sister and friend. When the new batch of girls arrived after two days of trekking from their village through the Sambisa to our camp, I did not care about their blistered soles and bruised skin. I did not care about their trancelike stares. I did not care about the girl still wearing remnants of her wedding dress. From the flower and spirogyra patterns painted on their arms and feet with *lalei* dye, I could tell which of the rest were her close friends and bridesmaids.

My only concern was that these girls were here to shorten my ration, that their coming meant more fierce battles around the food basin. And sure enough, the cornmeal has been all the more watery since they arrived. To feed more mouths, the broth must become less solid.

DEMOCRACY

"DEMOCRACY IS THE SYSTEM of infidels," Malam Adamu says. "Having anything to do with it is unbelief."

I wonder if Boko Haram has now managed to invade any more than the three northeast states from the fraction of the Nigerian map that Malam Zwindila shaded on the board.

I wonder if they have come any closer to toppling the democratically elected government of Nigeria.

I wonder if I will soon forget the definition of democracy, and everything else I learned in school.

GOD FORBID

WHAT IF BOKO HARAM attacked Mama on her way to or from Jalingo?

What if Mama is also dead?

I HAVE LOST COUNT

I HAVE LOST COUNT of the number of evenings and mornings we have been here. My mind has since stopped weighing me down with thoughts beyond one day at a time.

I arise each morning with no strength to think of tomorrow morning or the morning after tomorrow. I retire at night with no courage to think of tomorrow night or the night after tomorrow.

It strikes me like a hammer that Aisha could very well bring her baby into this world right here in the Sambisa forest. We could be here to see Malam Isa's first child begin its life without a father to give it a name.

We could be here till our bones turn brittle and our heads turn hoary.

We could be here until Jacob no longer remembers who I am.

RAIN

IT DROPS.

It pours.

It floods.

Soon, the dense branches, potent against the sun's rays, are powerless to shield us from the sky's tears.

For the first time since I came to the Sambisa, water washes the dirt from my body and from my clothes.

I am cold but clean.

CONVERSATIONS WITH ZAINAB

SOMETIMES, I WANT TO tell her to swat the fly perched on her lip, but I decide that there is no need.

Sometimes, I want to tell her that the cornrows I weaved on her head many days ago are shedding strands, but I realize that it does not matter.

Sometimes, I want to ask her if the baobab seed we planted together in her backyard may have sprouted by now, but I remember that it is no longer our business.

Sometimes, I want to show her that Al-Bakura has forgotten to zip up his fly, but I worry that the two of us might get our throats slashed for giggling.

Sometimes, I want to call her name to check whether she is sleeping or dead, but I fear that she may never answer.

RARE PRAISE

"WELL DONE," MALAM ADAMU says. "You're now ready to go on to the next step in becoming good Muslim women."

Even the worst student in the class is certified.

SNAKE

Aisha sees it first.

"Ahhh!" she screams.

It is slithering a footstep or two away from her bare feet, its long, green body almost blending with a nearby shrub.

"Snake! Snake!" we scream.

Women hop. Girls skip.

Everyone seems to think that the snake's brothers and sisters could be cocking their tails beneath their feet.

Quickly, I reach ahead for a branch and yank it from the nearest tree. But it is too straight. The snake could slide right up and inject its poison into my hand.

I reach for another branch, one with a forked end this time. Some girls grab stones big and small.

Within minutes, the beast is as flat as a *massa* cake, its head and tail several centimeters apart.

"This must be what I saw in my dream," Aisha says. "I dreamed that a big snake came and swallowed me whole, then it took my baby away and became its new mother."

What if another snake is hiding in the bushes?

What if it creeps out and swallows us while we are asleep?

I decide not to share my terror with her.

THE LEADER

IT IS CLEAR WHENEVER the mad man has returned.

The fresh flood of motorbikes.

The extended rows of trucks and Hilux vans.

The higher laundry pile of bloodied shirts and trousers.

The young men with hands and feet bound tightly with twine. Those of them who agree to join the Boko Haram jihad are taken away alive, still bound, in trucks or armored tanks. The others hear *"Allahu akbar!"* before their throats are slit in front of us by Al-Bakura, batch after batch, day by day.

But there is one sign that only the captives catch.

It is a sign that makes you almost wish that the Leader would stay in our camp forever, despite his fondness for a dagger.

Whenever the Leader is around, Al-Bakura and Malam Adamu do not tiptoe into our sleeping area at night. They leave the women to slumber in peace.

NO ESCAPE

AL-BAKURA IS IN OUR sleeping area. I am confused. The Leader arrived yesterday.

And it is not yet pitch-dark. Al-Bakura is not tiptoeing. He is striding from one end of our sleeping area to the other, accompanied by Amira, pointing from one girl to another.

"You!"

God does not answer my prayers. He points at me.

"You!"

I must flee.

But everywhere I look, trees, shrubs, and armed guards, many of whom cannot be more than a few years older than Jacob.

God help me.

A GIFT FROM ALLAH

"THESE ARE YOUR HUSBANDS," the Leader says. "Rijale, great fighters, commanders of this great army of Allah."

At first, his words do not make sense.

He points to the battalion of men sitting cross-legged at his right-hand side. None of them look familiar.

Maybe they arrived with him. Maybe this is all a dream, a new type of nightmare.

It is not.

Amira vanishes behind us. Malam Adamu steps forward to do the introductions.

"Husseina, this is your husband."

He points at a man with skin as light as condensed milk.

"Rabiyu, this is your husband."

He points at a man who is as bald-headed as an egg, with a beard as dense as the Sambisa.

"Maimuna, this is your husband."

He is short, the smallest of the entire battalion, like a full stop in the middle of a sentence.

On and on Malam Adamu goes until we have all met the men we are to marry on Friday. Zainab's groom has a thin, fresh scar running all the way from his right eye to the corner of his lip. Mine is wearing a cloth mask.

"These are the virgins that Allah has prepared for you," the Leader says.

I now know why the Boko Haram men have been tiptoeing and taking only the women. The rest of us have been preserved for the rijale. We are their reward for being brave murderers.

Right there and then, I decide that the land mines are a risk worth taking. Flee.

That is what I must do next.

RUN

WITHOUT MY CALENDAR TO assist me, I have lost count of the number of evenings and mornings that I have spent in this place, but one thing I know for sure is that Friday cannot be more than six days away. The sooner we make a break for it, the better.

"We must set off as soon as possible," I say.

"The land mines will blow us up," Zainab says.

"I'd rather get blown up than marry that man," I reply.

How can I get married to a man I do not know? Why does he keep his face covered? What does he have to hide?

In any case, whether he chooses to bury his face in a mask because it looks like a hippopotamus bottom or whether he is wary of dazzling damsels with his divine beauty, I do not want to marry him.

"Please, don't leave me here," Aisha says. "Please."

The size of her belly would make running impossible. But she isn't the one being forced to marry a Boko Haram fighter.

"I can't stay here. I can't get married. I would rather die," I say.

"But what if they catch us?" Zainab says.

"Whatever punishment they will inflict on us can't possibly be worse than forcing us to marry those men," I reply.

"Marriage may not be as bad as you think," Aisha says. "I

didn't know my husband before my parents decided that I should marry him. They chose him for me. But he turned out to be a good man."

"Your husband was not a member of Boko Haram," I reply, my tone harsher than I intended it to be.

Aisha is not deterred.

"At least you will get better food to eat," she says. "And your husbands will not let anyone whip you with a koboko. Also, they will allow you to sleep in their tents rather than out in the open."

Aisha's opinion is selfish, inspired by worry about being left behind rather than by our wishes and welfare. Nevertheless, she has a point. Marriage to Boko Haram has its advantages.

But, to a man who kills and maims for a living? Who does not believe in reading books? Whose home is inside the forest?

The thought is too lumpy for me to swallow. I shake my head from side to side.

Never.

"But where can someone have a wedding inside the forest?" Zainab asks.

I continue shaking my head.

"I don't know and I don't care."

"If you run away," Aisha says, "what will happen to Jacob? They may decide to get him from wherever he is and kill him as your punishment."

I stop shaking my head.

NEW LIFE

SUCCESS IS OFFICIATING AT my wedding to the man in a mask. I am about to say "I do."

"Argh!"

Aisha's scream jolts me awake from my nightmare. Zainab and everyone else are also awake. The moon is making its way back into its home in the sky.

Almost time for prayer.

"Ahhhh!"

We pull on our hijabs and hurry toward Aisha.

She clutches at twigs like a drowning man. She scratches the air like a woman possessed by demons. She is writhing her torso like a snake that has lost its head.

I kneel beside her. She grabs my arm and digs her nails into my skin.

"Ow!"

"Argh!" she replies.

"Aisha, what is the matter?" Zainab asks.

"Isa, look what you did to me!" she replies. "Isa, where are you? Look what you have done!"

My mind flashes back to the day Mama had Jacob.

"Her baby is coming!" I shriek.

One of the older girls pushes past us and raises Aisha's skirt.

"Jesus!"

"Argh!" Aisha screams.

"Push!" the woman says. "Push!"

Aisha takes a deep breath and contorts her face.

I hear the shrill cry of a newborn at the same time that Aisha heaves a deep sigh and closes her eyes.

"It's a boy," the woman says.

Aisha does not respond.

NEW MOTHER

AMIRA TICKLES HIS CHEEKS and kisses his lips and gibbers into his ears.

Zainab grabs Aisha's two hands while I take hold of her two legs. Her ankles are as bony as a camel's knees.

"Hurry up!" Al-Bakura says. "Stop wasting my time!"

Two Boko Haram men about Isaac's age stand waiting by the Hilux van.

We lay Aisha in the back of the vehicle, careful not to slam her body too hard against the white metal. She may be dead but she is still our friend, not a piece of firewood.

As the Boko Haram men drive Aisha's corpse away, I try to pick up the pieces of my shattered soul.

As Amira takes Malam Isa's first son away, I try to force my feet after her and grab my friend's child.

"At least Aisha is happier where she is," Zainab says, wiping her nose. "She is together with her husband."

At least the new baby will have better food than watery broth to eat, never mind that its new mother may not have any milk running from her nipples.

CONVERSATION WITH AISHA

"STOP WORRYING ABOUT YOUR breasts. All you need is to pray for a husband who likes them just the way they are. My husband told me that he doesn't want mine to grow any bigger. He likes them small so that he can cup them in his hands."

That was what she once told me, a secret about her and her husband, which I plan to take with me to my grave.

I never got around to asking her what it feels like to touch the hand of a man you love.

And now, I may never know.

TWO DAYS LATER

MY EYES HAVE STILL not shed a single tear for my precious friend Aisha.

NEW CLOTHES

Amira flings them at me.

A blouse and skirt of many colors with which to replace my rags, to change clothes for the first time in . . . how long?

And a black niqab.

FRIDAY

PAPA IS NOT HERE, no uncles are representing him, no extended family has been invited.

Who will accept the groom's proposal on my behalf?

Who will accept my bride price and gifts from the groom's family?

Where are the kola nuts, sweets, and bags of salt with which the groom's family will formally make their intentions known?

Where is his own extended family?

Dismal and silent, like a funeral procession, the new brides are led by Al-Bakura to the back of Hilux vans.

"Why are you not rejoicing for this great thing that Allah has done for you?" he asks. He laughs. "If you don't know it, you'd better know it now: your husbands are great men."

Soon, we are off to our new home in the forest, to our husbands' lairs.

Leaving Aisha's dead body behind. Leaving Malam Isa's newborn son behind.

How will Jacob know where to find me?

On this ugliest of days, my heart rejoices at its straw of happy news when Zainab and I are placed inside the same van.

And may I never set eyes on Al-Bakura ever again.

. . . For having left, in the Caliph's kitchen,
Of a nest of scorpions no survivor,—
With him I proved no bargain-driver,
With you, don't think I'll bate a stiver!
And folks who put me in a passion
May find me pipe after another fashion . . .

—Robert Browning, "The Pied Piper of Hamelin"

FANNE

ON HER FINGERS, WRISTS, and ankles, Fanne displays more glittering jewelry than Amira did. She welcomes us with a steaming basin of white rice and tomato stew. I have never been more grateful for a meal. I keep expecting to wake up and discover that it was all a dream, the aroma disappearing into hot air.

With my spirit, soul, and body immersed in the rice and stew, not once do I remember Jacob or Mama or Papa or my brothers. I forget that Zainab is by my side.

My mind is consumed with pushing more and more of the rice down my throat. The one blot on my enjoyment is worry about how long the food will last before the basin is empty.

"You will be happy here," Fanne says. "Your husbands are brave men. They will take good care of you."

TWO DROPS OF WATER

THE DIFFERENCE BETWEEN THIS new camp and the previous one is the difference between a drop of sewer water and a drop of puddle water.

I am still inside the Sambisa forest, shrubs and trees everywhere. The Boko Haram men are all over the place, like maggots in rotten fruit.

But at night, I do not sleep under a tree.

I do not put up with insects clamping their jaws into my skin.

I do not imagine crustaceans and creepy crawlies beneath my mattress of twigs.

I do not panic each time the sky changes from blue to gray.

I do not shiver while the rain drenches my clothes and seeps into my bones, or while the wind screams and slashes my face.

I do not hear the weak ones among us wheezing and coughing till dawn.

I do not wake to find someone two bodies away from mine frozen in her sleep.

I do not wonder whether I will be among those chosen to ferry the frigid corpse to a Hilux van, so that the Boko Haram men can bury it beneath a baobab tree.

No.

In this new camp, I am free of all that.

I am to sleep inside a tarpaulin tent that has a flat mattress on the floor and a thin flap covering the entrance and a dim electric bulb hanging from the low roof.

And the man in a mask.

THE FIRST TIME

THROUGH THE WINDOW OF my niqab, I watch him watching me through the two holes in his mask. My heart slams against my chest.

His eyes are sharp, each like a pin. His legs are stretched out in front of him on the mattress. He is long and lean.

His upper half is in a brown singlet. His lower half is in camouflage trousers.

What is he hiding behind the mask?

His eyes travel from my head to my heel, making a brief stopover at my chest. His eyes travel back from my heel to my head, making yet another brief stopover at my chest.

And then the voices start playing in my head.

Mama's voice.

"You are a woman. From now on, you must be very careful of men. You must never allow a man to touch you."

Principal's voice.

"To boys, you are just like a trout darting about in the stream. They have their rod and line in hand, waiting to catch any fish that is foolish enough to bite the bait instead of leaping out of the way."

Pastor Moses's voice.

"The Bible tells us that the devil goes about like a roaring lion, seeking whom to devour. Women, be sober, be vigilant. The devil, the devourer, will often come to you in the form of a man."

And here I am with a man, an angler, a predator. Alone. Stooped in his tent. At night.

Like a rabbit fleeing a fox, I turn around and take to my heels. I dash through the thin flap of the tent.

Something obstructs my passage. I push. I shove. The something pushes and shoves back.

Fanne.

Legs astride and bottom curved backward, she barricades my exit route.

My blood bubbles with panic. The man in the mask rises and takes a step toward me.

I scream.

I flee in the opposite direction, toward the big, black gun resting on a pair of boots.

He follows. I leap over the mattress. I stumble on a Quran.

He grabs a handful of my niqab and pulls me into his arms. I scream.

He throws me on the mattress. I pick myself up and scramble away from his feet.

He grabs my shoulder and flips me over.

LAST NIGHT

I KEEP SHOVING IT out of my mind.

I keep shutting my eyes to make it disappear.

At last, I force the memory into a cage and bolt it with a metal padlock, then fling the key deep into Lake Chad.

DELICIOUS

I AM STANDING WITH my best friend after our first set of Quranic classes, when her husband, Ali, walks past us with other rijale.

He stops.

For an alarming second, his hand hovers so close to hers that I worry he is about to touch her in public.

He lowers his head and coos like a mother talking to her month-old girl.

"You're a delicious woman," he says. "Has anyone ever told you that before? You're the most delicious woman I have ever known."

A smile creeps into Zainab's eyes. It disappears almost immediately.

No.

I must have imagined it.

ADVICE

MY MISSION IS TO ensure that my husband is always happy and well.

"If he is angry, you also will be angry," Fanne says. "Your duty is to make sure that he is always happy, so that you also will be happy."

I do not know if I remember what it feels like to be happy. I do not know if I will ever feel happiness again.

But I do know that bucking will not relieve a donkey of its burden. As long as the animal is tethered to its owner, he will simply place the load back on the donkey again.

SILVER

My heart somersaults when I see it.

From underneath his pile of folded shirts, it peeps.

Should I? Should I not?

The temptation is too hard to resist.

Hands shivering, I reach for the silver metal and run my fingers along the smooth edge.

My new husband owns a laptop.

I wonder if Success is thinking about me right now. I wonder if he misses our little chats. I wonder if he will be devastated to learn that I now belong to another man.

LIFE OF A WIFE

FETCH WATER.

Wash clothes.

Wipe boots.

Cook.

Wash dishes.

Tidy tent.

Lie in the dark and wait.

I am no longer a slave of Boko Haram. I am the slave of only one man.

OSAMA

IT IS DIFFERENT FROM the name with which Malam Adamu declared him my husband.

It must be a name he chose for himself.

It is certainly not a Hausa name.

It does not sound like an English name.

What, then, could it be? Or mean?

Maybe this name by which other rijale hail my husband is Arabic.

Maybe it is a Muslim name that I have never heard before.

Maybe it is a name he made up from his favorite vowels and consonants, just because he likes the sound.

SCAR

"HE TOLD ME THAT a Nigerian soldier tried to kill him with a sword," Zainab says. "But he overpowered the soldier with his bare hands and broke his neck."

Zainab knows how Ali got the thin, fresh scar running all the way from his right eye to the corner of his lip. I still don't know why Osama wears a mask.

"He said there's no single soldier in the entire Nigerian army that can fight him and win," Zainab adds.

Zainab has conversations with Ali, never mind that he seems to do all the talking while she does the listening. Osama has no time for any utterance other than matrimonial commands.

MESMERIZED

HE ROLLS OFF ME and flips the silver gadget open on his lap. I lie still.

His fingers fly across the keypad, tapping and clicking. Surely using a laptop cannot be as complicated as I had imagined? If only I had asked Success to teach me how to turn it on.

A picture comes up on the screen. He clicks. It moves.

A crowd of barefoot ragamuffins is gathered in front of a Boko Haram flag, knives and guns hanging from their fingers. The next scene shows the boys scatting and screaming, waving their guns and knives in the air. Another scene shows one of the boys stepping forward to stand beside the Leader, who has his right foot on the head of a man whose hands and feet are bound. At the Leader's command, the boy applies his knife. Blood gushes from the man's throat.

"Ahh . . ."

I swallow my shock just in time. Still, my husband must have heard. Watching Boko Haram men slash throats is quite a different sight from watching a boy of Jacob's age do the same thing. I close my eyes tight and wait for him to bark at me for watching his laptop in the dark.

But my husband says nothing. All he does is click.

Another video.

Men in green camouflage uniforms speed about in an armored tank, firing guns at random into the air. They leap off the vehicle and plant the black and white Boko Haram flag in front of a building with a sign that reads "Gwoza Local Government Authority." Then, they set fire to the green-white-green Nigerian national flag and cheer.

"Allah be praised," my husband says.

He flips his laptop shut and returns it beneath his pile of clothes, then stretches his elbows and knees across three-quarters of the mattress.

Those vicious little boys in the video must be the beastly offspring of Boko Haram.

SINGING

As I approach Zainab's tent, which is about ten tarpaulin residences away from mine, the sound of singing stops me in my tracks.

A man's voice.

A Hausa song.

A lovestruck beau to the sole object of his total affections, whom he describes as the other half of his soul.

"*Na so ki*
Rabin raina
Domin halinki ya ah
Shi ne ni ke so . . ."

MIND OF A FLY

A COCONUT AND A handful of date fruits, from Fanne to each of the new wives converged around her.

"We are running low on tea," she says. "But don't worry. When the brave fighters go out for their next jihad, they will bring us back more food."

Like two lumps of dung that confuse the mind of a fly, I struggle to decide whether being married is better than being a slave.

LAUGHING

FANNE'S CHILD CRAWLS AWAY from the party of romping toddlers. After inspecting a rough stone closely, he proceeds on his journey and stops at my feet.

He holds my gaze with his wide, brown eyes, almond-shaped and innocent, a far cry from the malevolence in his rijale father's glare.

He laughs.

Perplexed by the source of his humor, I recall Jacob's frequent giggling when playing with his lizards. I smile and tickle the boy's chin.

I wonder if Jacob has captured some new lizards to play with wherever he is.

The baby keeps laughing. Soon, three more toddlers are guffawing along with him, like a pack of hyenas.

I lift him by the armpits and place him in my lap.

Only a child clueless that he is in the thick of the forest surrounded by murderers and misery can find reason to laugh.

SHOWING OFF

"Look," Zainab says.

On her wrist is a silver bangle.

"Look," she says.

On her pinkie is a pink, plastic ring.

"My husband gave them to me," she says.

Some birds avoid water while the duck revels in it. Whenever he is out of sight, I try my best to wipe my husband from my mind. But not Zainab.

"He told me that I have the most beautiful hands in the world," she says, fluttering her eyelashes and smiling at her ring.

If only Zainab could transmit some of her newfound bliss to me. If only she could infect my eyes with the twinkle in hers.

"My husband lets me watch his laptop," I say.

HIS FAVORITE

TONIGHT, MY HUSBAND WATCHES his favorite video, the one he likes to play over and over again, night after night.

I know the scenes by heart.

The airplane flies from the right-hand side toward the two tall buildings that look as if they are touching the sky. When it seems like the pilot will finally come to his senses and veer left, he drives straight on.

A cloud of fire. A cyclone of crushed cement.

And then a second airplane.

And then the two towers vanish.

"Allah be praised," my husband says.

BUTTERMINT

"HERE, HAVE ONE," ZAINAB says. "My husband gave them to me."

"Oh! Thank you!"

I never imagined that I would enjoy a Buttermint sweet ever again.

NEW STRENGTH

WITH MY STOMACH CONSTANTLY filled with different foods and the strength restored to my muscles and bones, a long-forgotten thought limps back into my mind.

"It could be easier for us to escape now that we're married," I say. "Maybe we could hide in the back of one of the Hilux vans. They don't watch us as closely as they did before."

Zainab says nothing.

"I wonder how far into the forest we are," I say. "They may not have as many land mines around here as they did where they kept us as slaves."

Zainab says nothing.

MEMORIES

AFTER MY HUSBAND PULLS on his mask and leaves with his gun, I dream. But no matter how hard I try, my mind cannot conjure up any visions of the future. All I see are pictures from the past.

I remember my first day of school. Prancing behind Papa in my brand-new white blouse and blue pinafore, clutching my new exercise books and pencil. At the headmaster's office, Papa waited in the queue until my full name had been entered in the register, then he turned to me and smiled.

"Make sure you study hard so that one day you can teach me how to read and write," he said. He smiled. "And maybe how to speak English, as well."

I remember Jacob's naming ceremony. Papa had bought a ram for the special occasion. He and Abraham spent the entire day butchering and barbecuing. Mama popped into the backyard with the suckling baby at her nipple, apprehensive that the ram meat would not go around.

"Cut it smaller. Cut it smaller," she said. "The pieces are too large."

One week of tethering the ram to the veranda and feeding it shoots and leaves had profited little. It could easily have passed for a lamb, but that was the best Papa's pocket could do. Thankfully, all the guests who attended the celebration ended up with a piece of mutton atop their mounds of *jollof* rice, never mind that some of the cuts were as miniature as sugar cubes.

I remember Pastor Moses's blue car. Because he was the only man in our village who owned a vehicle that could travel far without its engine giving up halfway down the highway, Pastor Moses was paid some money by the government so that he could ferry any woman in labor to the hospital in Gwoza. But he was away in Damaturu the weekend Jacob was born. Papa had to send for Hajia Turai, who had handled mine and many other births in the village long before the local government officials started telling everyone that all the mothers and babies who died during childbirth would have lived if they had gone to a hospital instead of doing it themselves at home.

I remember Papa's story about a greedy girl from the Fulani tribe. "She never stopped eating," he said. "She would eat even the earth from under your feet." One day, when she had eaten everything within sight and had nothing left to eat, she came across seven dogs at a bend in the road. Quickly, she swallowed them all. "The next time she opened her mouth to say good afternoon," he said, "she barked like a dog. For the rest of her life, she barked instead of talked."

I remember Isaac laughing. Once in a while, he caught a lizard in the backyard and imprisoned it inside a transparent plastic bag, then shackled the bag to Jacob's wrist with twine. As Jacob dragged the twine about, the lizard wriggled and writhed, while Isaac and Jacob applauded and laughed.

I remember Abraham in the boxing ring. He had heard how much the local *dambe* boxers were paid per match and decided to give it a try. On the first Saturday of the holidays, we all went to watch his first fight. Naked apart from a pair of denim knee-length shorts and the string around his hands that served as gloves, he paced around the school field with fury in his eyes. But as soon as he met Babandogo in the middle of the field and Babandogo's fist met with Abraham's face, the fight came to a quick end.

I remember Malam Zwindila's lessons about Nigeria's independence from Britain. "Many brave Nigerians worked hard to make sure that our great country became free from the white man's rule," he said. There was even a woman among the brave men, called Margaret Ekpo.

I remember Mama. But each time I see her, all the beautiful pictures from the past turn to ashes. She is rolling on the floor in tears.

WATCHING MEN

"THAT GUN HE IS holding is an RPG," Zainab says. "It can destroy an armored tank hundreds of meters away. He told me it is the same kind of gun used by jihad fighters in other countries around the world."

The gun, thin and long with each end shaped like a cylinder, looks like Mama's wooden pestle for pounding condiments. Appearances can be deceiving.

"He told me that he started with only a single knife," she says. "But today, thanks be to Allah, he has hundreds of guns and more than twenty armored vehicles under his command."

I know how the rijale get their wives.

I know how the rijale get their food.

I wonder how the rijale get their guns.

LIKE MALAM ZWINDILA

APART FROM THE QURAN, there are many other things that a Boko Haram wife needs to learn. Sometimes, the training classes feel almost like attending a real school, except without notepaper and pen.

Fanne walks to and fro between the rows of Boko Haram wives sitting on the floor, hands on her hips or behind her back.

Like Malam Zwindila.

She allows us to ask her questions about anything that we do not understand.

She asks us questions to make sure we understand.

She makes us cheer with "Glory be to Allah" when a girl answers a question right. Clapping hands, Malam Adamu taught us, is forbidden in Islam, another haram. Muslim women are allowed to clap only when calling the Imam's attention if he makes an error while leading prayers. Men must not clap at all.

Some of the rijale sit in on our training sessions and promise us the opportunity to leave the Sambisa forest one day to practice all that we have learned.

"Allah does not allow men to fight women," Fanne says. "In the jihad, you brave women of brave fighters have to be the ones to fight infidel women for Allah."

BUGLE

THE FRESH FLOOD OF motorbikes.

The extended rows of trucks and Hilux vans.

The mad man is around.

For hours and hours, right into the night, the rijale converge around him.

"We must spread our message by teaching and by sword!" he says. "We must make a river for Allah with the blood of infidels!"

His bugle compels me to stay awake, to join the rijale and listen to his gory words.

JIHAD

HALF A BASIN OF date fruits.

One sack of millet.

Five coconuts.

Twelve sacks of groundnuts.

That is all the food we have left. The portions now have to be rationed.

When the meal is over, the children clutch at their mothers' niqabs and wail for more.

I wish the rijale would hurry off to their next jihad, so that they can bring us back more looted food.

OUTSIDE WORLD

Do PEOPLE STILL GO to the farm, dig ridges, plant roots and seeds, cover them with mulch and manure?

Do people still go to the market, haggle over the price of fish and tomatoes, roam from stall to stall in search of the best deal?

Do children still jump into the streets and sing when the sky thunders and the clouds prepare to release, stamp their feet in mud and splash about in puddles?

Does Pastor Moses still preach on Sundays, shout his sermon and alter the inflection of his voice to emphasize a point?

I do not want to think about Mama.

LUCKY BRIDE

"YOU MUST TRY TO stop thinking all the time," Zainab says. "Try to be happy. This is the life we have now."

Easy for her to say.

Every day, her husband stops by the training tent to ask if Zainab is getting on fine.

Always, he flashes her a grin when he walks past with other rijale.

Sometimes, he saves her a piece of bush meat from the men's meal.

Zainab can afford to be happy because she is not married to the man in the mask.

GOOD LOOKS

HE ROLLS OFF ME and soon begins to snore.

I bore my gaze through the dim light of the moon, scanning his body from head to foot. The only opportunity I have to stare him straight in the face.

Long lashes. Pointed nose. Thick lips. High cheekbones.

From the Kanuri tribe, perhaps.

So, why does he choose to keep his good looks concealed?

Why does he hide his features behind a ghastly cloth? Does he look the same out in daylight as he does in the dim light inside?

Would I recognize him if I saw him outside the tent without his mask?

TRYING TO BE HAPPY

MAYBE MY HUSBAND WATCHES these videos for my benefit.

Maybe he not only knows that I am watching along with him, but he also wants me to watch.

Maybe in his own special way, he loves me as much as Zainab's husband loves her.

A NEW FRIEND

ZAINAB PLAITS FANNE'S HAIR.

Fanne whispers into Zainab's ears.

Zainab giggles.

Fanne gives Zainab an extra palmful of date fruits.

Zainab shares some of the dates with me.

DECISION

ZAINAB LISTENED PATIENTLY WHENEVER I mused over Success.

Zainab shared my excitement whenever he visited and my disappointment whenever he did not.

Now that Zainab has found someone to love, I also must listen patiently and share in her joy.

It will be difficult. But, as her best friend, I must try.

GOSSIP

"I ASKED HER AGAIN and she said she still doesn't know," Zainab says. "Nobody knows exactly why your husband chooses to wear a mask all the time."

"Can Fanne not ask her husband?"

"He may wonder why she's asking about another woman's husband and get upset."

True.

Pity that my husband never shares his heart with me.

Pity that I have to resort to other people's mouths to discover the thoughts that might be lurking in his mind.

Pity that he is not like Success, who had time for all my questions and who was going to give me storybooks that would lead to more questions and more answers.

"Maybe he has a mentor who also wears a mask," Zainab suggests. "Fanne said he asked everyone to start calling him Osama because of a great warrior for Allah who was also called by that name. The great man was killed by infidels. Your husband adores him."

At least one mystery is solved.

IN-LAWS

Her eyes are dark.

Her face is cloudy.

Her hand is holding up her chin.

For a change, Zainab is unhappy in her new life. I wonder if this is how despondent I look all the time, like a hen drenched in the rain.

I sit beside her on the mat and place my arm around her shoulder.

"What's the matter?" I ask.

"My period began this morning," she says.

Has she started feeling the cramps? Is she out of fresh rags? Did her husband push her to the edge of the mattress with his feet as mine does whenever I am menstruating and too unclean to be useful to him?

"I'd thought I was pregnant," she says.

"Pregnant? You wanted to be pregnant?"

"My husband promised that he would take me with him to visit Maiduguri, but only after I give him a child."

"Maiduguri? What are you going there to do?"

"His mother lives there," she replies. "I was looking forward to meeting my in-laws."

It is difficult, but I must try.

STILL WONDERING ABOUT IT

BEING STUCK IN THE forest forever with the Boko Haram beasts, or getting pregnant with a Boko Haram beast for a chance to see the outside world.

Which option is better?

TRAINING

"WHEN YOU SEE SOLDIERS from the Nigerian army, confront them," Fanne says. "Never be afraid. Nothing will happen to you."

She makes it sound as easy as killing rats with a stick.

"We women must learn from our husbands," she says. "They are giving their blood for the cause. We also must go to war for Allah."

A NEW TEACHER

"Boko Haram are not really bad people," she says. "They are only trying to change the world for Allah."

My ears cannot believe what they are hearing.

"They may be killing people now, but it is so that we can have peace and live under Sharia law," she says.

My eyes check, but there is no sign of jest in her face.

"The way many people in Nigeria are living, Allah is not happy about it. That's why they decided to do something about it."

These are the words of my best friend, Zainab.

"That's what my husband told me," she says.

ARGUMENT

THIS TIME, MY TONGUE does not abandon me because of shock. I respond instantly to her rubbish words.

"Zainab, how can you even think to say that they are doing this for Allah? Have you forgotten Aisha? Have you forgotten Malam Isa? Is this the same Allah they worshiped?"

She puckers her lips tight like a turkey's bottom.

"Boko Haram has nothing to do with Islam," I say. Falling for a man is one thing; denying evil is another altogether. "They are just evil human beings. There is nothing good or godly about Boko Haram."

She is quiet. She shrugs.

"My husband is a good man," she says.

GROWING UP

THE CHILDREN SHRIEK AND squeak in pursuit of a squirrel that has peeked through a shrub by the cooking area. The rodent escapes and they follow its bushy tail behind the trees.

When the children grow, they will know everything about the forest and about the Quran and about artillery.

When the children grow, they will know nothing about flipping the pages of a new book or sitting on a bus while the world flits past through the windows or playing football against the neighboring village school's team.

TATTOO

"COME AND SEE," ZAINAB says to me.

I follow her into her husband's tent. His Quran is lying open on the mattress.

She stands in a corner and lifts her niqab and then her blouse.

"Argh!" I scream.

"Shhhhhhh!" she says.

Her flesh is raw and red.

"Who did this to you?" I ask.

"My husband," she replies, smiling. "It's his name."

Indeed, it is the name *Ali*, spelled in Arabic. Malam Adamu would be proud to see that all his teaching was not in vain. I can read Arabic.

"Isn't it painful?"

"He told me that, with his name tattooed on my stomach, everyone would know that I belong to him, even if he doesn't return from the jihad."

It is difficult, but I must try.

FOR THE FIFTH DAY IN A ROW

I ENTER THE TENT at night with no tightness in my stomach.

I sprawl on the mattress and spread my arms far apart.

I shut my eyes and snooze, not worrying that my sleep may be cut short in the morning if he awakes and wants his wife immediately.

This jihad that has taken my husband away from the camp? May it last forever.

FONDER

"HE TOLD ME THAT he used to be a fisherman near Lake Chad," she says.

"He told me that his older brother is also a rijale, in another camp," she says.

"He told me that, one day, he will take me with him to paradise," she says.

In Ali's absence, Zainab's heart grows fonder. From dawn till dusk, she talks about nothing else. As she speaks, she stares into the sky ahead of her, smiling at the sun.

I know nothing about my husband's past. The videos are the only stories he shares with me. Sometimes, I suspect that he would rather be alone, that, like me, he was forced to take a spouse.

DAY SEVENTEEN

MAYBE HE'S DEAD.

Will I be allowed to live in the tent by myself?

Will they marry me off to someone else?

Will my new husband be in this camp or in another camp?

Will he be a good husband like Zainab's, or will he be even better?

Will he be proud to know that I won a Borno State government scholarship for exceptional children from disadvantaged homes?

Will he allow me to go to school?

TODAY'S LESSON

How TO HOLD, COCK, fire, and clean an unloaded gun. "The faster, the better," Fanne says.

How to set roofs alight and throw firebombs through open windows. "Aim for the thatch, which easily catches fire," she says.

How to rush into buildings and backyards while the men are shooting. "Cart off all the jewelry, clothes, and foodstuff you see," she says.

GOSSIP

"No, no," Zainab whispers. "Fanne has more than two children. She told me so herself. Her oldest child is in the boot camp where children learn how to become brave fighters for Allah."

"But I thought you said she's been married for just five years," I say.

"Yes. Her oldest son is four."

"Four?"

"Lower your voice!"

"Isn't he too young?"

"It's never too young to start bringing up the children who will keep the work of Allah going even after our brave husbands go to paradise."

Surely Zainab can't really believe this?

"Is that what you would want for your own child?" I ask.

"It's not about what I want. It is about what Allah wants."

"Are you trying to tell me that Allah would rather have these children fighting than being in school and learning new things every day? Does it mean that—"

"We cannot question the will of Allah."

"Allah can't possibly—"

"No matter how intelligent we think we are, remember that Allah knows best."

MY INTELLIGENCE

IT MADE ME THE pride of Papa and Principal.

It saved me from Malam Zwindila's lashings.

It won me the Borno State government scholarship.

Could it now be causing me misery, preventing me from believing, and enjoying my new life?

A sack full of precious stones will only slow down your trek through the wilderness, after all, and is better dumped by the wayside or exchanged for a cup of water.

FINISHED

No BREAKFAST, NO LUNCH, no dinner.

Nothing left to eat until the men return.

DAY THIRTY-TWO

MY SWEET DREAMS ARE in smithereens at my feet.

He does not wait till nighttime.

As soon as the rijale disembark from the trucks and vans, he beckons me to the tent and shuts the flap.

He pulls off his bloodstained shirt and jumps on top of me.

VICTORY

"THEY HAVE TAKEN OVER more towns," Zainab says. "They now rule more than half of Borno."

She smacks her hands together in excitement.

"Very soon, Boko Haram will be the only government that Nigeria knows. He told me so himself."

COMFORTER

For a change, my husband has left me enough space on the mattress.

He is crouched like a fetus in bed, his knees squeezed into his stomach and his arms tight against his chest, his back curved toward me.

He is sniffling.

As I lie beside him and listen, I reflect on the instruction Fanne gave me earlier in the day.

"You must try and comfort him as much as you can. His father and mother have been killed by infidels. The Nigerian army bombed their house in Michika."

Was his father also a member of Boko Haram? Or was he an innocent man killed while listening to his radio at home?

Was his mother aware that her son was married to a stolen girl?

Was he sporting a mask whenever he dropped by and she served him sizzling *kosai* straight from the fire, with fresh *fura da nono*?

I do not know the answer to these questions, and Fanne does not offer any additional information. What I do know for certain is the pain of losing a father you loved, of watching him drop to the floor never to rise again.

But how can I comfort my husband?

How does one comfort a brave fighter? How does one comfort a rijale? How does one comfort a Boko Haram man?

How does one draw blood from a stone?

At a loss for ideas, I sit up in bed and stare at his back, worried that Fanne will ask me about it tomorrow, and tell me off if I have not been a good wife.

Tentatively, I stretch out my hand. It hovers above his shoulder. Gradually, I let it down. Eventually, it touches his skin.

He does not bite my fingers. He does not fling my hand away in anger. He does not bark at me to disappear.

I pat his shoulder.

Once. Twice. Thrice.

Suddenly, he grabs my hand.

He squeezes it tight and holds it firmly against his chest. Then he draws me into his arms and weeps into my neck.

Before I can stop myself, I am crying.

I am not sure why.

I am not sure if my tears are for his fresh grief or for mine that has crystallized.

Or maybe I am just weeping from relief.

MORNING AFTER

HE RATTLES ME AWAKE.

He shoves me out of his arms.

He barks for his shirt and his boots.

He asks why I am standing there like an idiot.

He commands me to get out of his sight.

My husband is once again the brave fighter he was before last night.

SPOILS OF WAR

FANNE DISTRIBUTES THE NEW blouses and skirts.

Mine is blue, with small yellow elephants. Zainab gets a purple one with black polka dots.

I wonder if the girl who owned the dress managed to escape to the hills or if she ended up in a Sambisa camp.

I wonder who might have inherited my red dress and Zainab's shiny black shoes.

BRACELET

"Look!" Zainab says. "He told me that this one is made of pure gold!"

THROUGH THE WINDOW
OF MY NIQAB

THEY CLUTCH EACH OTHER'S hands tight.

They cringe when the Leader speaks.

They creep around their secluded area, carved out for just enough room to sleep and to sit up and learn the Quran.

I wonder how long it will take before these new slaves that have accompanied our husbands back from jihad will shed their body fat, how long before their nice skirts start shedding thread.

CAUTION

"WE HAVE TO BE careful to treat our husbands especially well now that these new girls have arrived," Zainab says, "otherwise, they might decide to marry another girl."

That is what Fanne told her.

BOARDING SCHOOL

A BOOK ON MY lap, two at my feet, dozens lining the shelves around me.

A bell rings and I know it is time to go to my next class.

Instead, I wake up from sleep.

EXPERT

I KNOW HOW TO pretend that I am not there while he does what he pleases with my body.

I know how to forget that I am lying beside a naked man whose papa and mama and brothers and sisters I do not know.

I know how to hold a gun and shoot. I can grab my husband's gun and blow his brains out while he is still snoring, before he has the time to roll over and open his eyes.

And then what?

My heart beats faster, and my toes curl tighter.

I am afraid of leaving the Sambisa.

Here, I know how each day will begin.

I know that I will say my prayers five times. I know that I will cook and wash and clean from dawn till dusk. I know that five days every month, I will be too unclean to come before my husband or before Allah. I know that Fanne will remind me if I forget to do any of the things I am supposed to do.

But I have no idea what might be waiting for me outside the Sambisa. I have no clue how to navigate the new world out there.

A world with no Papa and no brothers. And maybe with no Mama.

How will Mama and her brothers and sisters receive the

news that I am married to a Muslim man whose family I do not know? How will Pastor Moses react? How will Salamatu survive in a world she has never experienced before?

Maybe inside the Sambisa forest is better. Maybe the life I know is better than the one I do not know. Maybe my dreams of a different life are just a waste of time.

SPECIAL VEST

"Who wants to be the first person to try on the special vest?" Fanne asks.

Hands shoot up in the air. I also raise my hand. Fanne's eyes scour the room.

"Zainab," she says.

Zainab moves to the front, a smile on her face and a new bracelet on her left wrist.

After Zainab tries on the special vest, Fanne invites the rest of us to take our turns. One after the other, we stand and move to the front.

"Nobody will notice it under your niqab," she says. "If they do, they will think you are pregnant. They won't search you because they know it's against your honor for them to touch a woman."

When Fanne slips the vest across my waist and buckles it tightly at the back, I feel as if I am carrying three sacks of millet.

The belt has several cylinders attached to it, and some wires sticking out here and there.

"This is where you must pull," Fanne says. "But you must remember to first recite the Sura Albakara as you do so. Immediately, you will see millions of angels and money. You will find yourself in paradise."

I wonder if the paradise the rijale and Fanne have been telling us about is the same paradise that Pastor Moses often talked about.

The same paradise where clear waters gushed and streets were paved with gold, where everything was strange and new. Sparrows were brighter than peacocks, dogs outran deer, bees lost their stings, horses were born with eagle's wings. Lame feet were cured and blind eyes were opened. No sorrow, no tears, no pain or death.

"Only special ones chosen by Allah can carry out this task in the jihad," Fanne says. "Only special ones can arrive in paradise so quickly and easily."

GOLD RING

"By the grace of Allah, Boko Haram will one day rule Nigeria," Zainab says.

No matter how hard I try, how far away I shove my intelligence, I still don't understand.

"But why do they have to kill people?" I ask. "Why do they have to rape women and force girls to marry them?"

She snorts and looks away at her gold ring.

Ali may be a good husband to Zainab, but he is certainly not a good Muslim.

BOYS

ONE BY ONE, THE young fighters step forward.

One by one, the Leader issues an instruction.

One by one, each boy recites a Quran passage, fires a gun at a piece of wood, slashes a man's throat.

One boy stands out from the rest.

Something about the way he runs forward. Something about the way he crooks his neck. Something about his eyes, his nose, his . . .

This cannot be.

I shine my eyes brighter.

"Ah—!"

I swallow my scream.

My husband clicks to another video.

JACOB

"I SAW JACOB ON my husband's laptop," I say. "He's alive. I saw him with my own eyes."

"Allah be praised!" Zainab says.

"But the Boko Haram men have turned him into one of them. I wish I knew where the place is so that I can go and get him out."

"You should thank Allah that he's still alive. He is going to grow up to be a brave fighter. Like our husbands."

"There is nothing brave about this jihad! They are all monsters! Killers and murderers! Every single one of them! Including Ali! Allah will send them all to burn in hell! They are traitors to their faith. They are a criminal group. Their sickening deeds show that they have nothing in common with other Muslims like Malam Isa, Malam Shettima, and Aisha, and that they lack respect for the religion they claim to fight for!"

Silence.

And then she stands.

"May Allah forgive you your blasphemy," Zainab says.

She walks away, leaving me alone with my grief.

TWO HUSBANDS

THERE IS THE MAN in the mask who stomps around the camp, barking commands and firing weapons for fun, who makes me wish that every member of Boko Haram would burn in hell.

There is the man who knows that I am secretly watching the videos on his laptop with him but who does not seem to mind, who makes me wish that the worldwide jihad would be successful so that all the killing will stop and we can all live happily ever after in peace.

Maybe the second man would be willing to listen if I ask him in the dark.

Maybe his looks are deceitful like cow dung, hard on the outside and soft on the inside.

Maybe he will let me go and visit Jacob if I ask him the location of the boys' training camp in his video.

BLASPHEMY

My husband stomps into the tent.

He flings his gun on the mattress. His gaze is crimson red.

Without a word, he reaches for my niqab and grabs a handful.

His fists land on my head, my neck, my stomach. The entire Sambisa must hear my screams.

His boots dig into my shins, my knees, my back. Like the man who falls down a well and seizes the edge of a sword to keep himself from going farther down, I shout for help.

"Fanne! Fanne! Please, come and save me!"

The most powerful woman I know does not appear.

"Next time you blaspheme the name of Allah," he says, "I will kill you. I will chop your body in pieces."

He flings me on the bed and jumps on me.

BETRAYAL

THE BANGING PAIN IN my head.

The throbbing pain in my neck.

The stinging pain in between my legs.

All these pale in comparison to the clawing in my heart, the pain of betrayal by my best friend.

DISGRACED

THE OTHER WIVES STOP speaking when I approach.

Some glare at me and snort.

When their children crawl toward my feet, they scramble forward and grab them away.

"You should be ashamed of yourself," Fanne says. "Your husband is a great fighter and you are behaving like an infidel, making nasty comments about Allah. The Leader will soon find him a better wife and you can go back to being a slave."

OLD FRIEND

ZAINAB PLAITS FANNE'S HAIR.

Fanne whispers into Zainab's ears.

Zainab giggles.

Fanne gives Zainab an extra palmful of groundnuts.

Zainab does not share the groundnuts with me.

THINKING ABOUT ZAINAB

MY BLOOD BOILS.

My chest tightens.

My mind wishes she would trip on a stone and break her neck.

Maybe it is hatred. Maybe it is jealousy.

Maybe I just want my best friend back.

PARADISE

THE CLASS IS SILENT while Fanne makes her announcement.

"Zainab, your husband wants you to be the first one to go to jihad. Will you accept this great honor?"

She smiles. Fanne smiles.

Now, I know for sure what I feel toward my friend.

Jealousy.

Zainab just seems to have all the good luck in the world. Here I am, stuck in the Sambisa forest for the rest of my life, with a husband who despises me and women who scorn me, while she gets to go with the men and see the outside world.

"Two of our bravest rijale will take you to the place," she says. "Your husband will also go with you. He will give you the vest to wear and tell you everything you need to do."

What? The vest that sends people to paradise?

I am not so jealous of Zainab anymore. I want to jump up and beg her to please not go!

SUPERSTAR

"WE ARE PROUD OF YOU," some say.

"Congratulations," others say.

"I always knew you were special," yet others say.

From the little food we have left, Zainab receives the lion's share.

Each time I approach her, she is surrounded by dozens of women, whose glares dare the blasphemer to come any closer.

I MUST TRY

THEIR GLARES DARE THE blasphemer to come any closer.

I ignore them and set my focus on Zainab.

Heart pounding, I rush forward and clutch her niqab.

"Zainab! Zainab!"

She turns.

"Please, don't go! Please! You won't—"

A slap on my face. Two more. Another on my back.

"Get away from her!" Fanne says. "You wretched infidel."

HEARTBROKEN

HAVING NOT SEEN HER for the past two days, I know she must have gone.

My best friend has left for paradise. Without bothering to tell me good-bye.

BOOM

THIS TIME, I KNOW that it is not the clapping of distant thunder.

It is also not a nightmare, because the floor around me is not slimy with fresh intestines, and Papa and Isaac are not drowning in puddles of blood.

It is not the blasting of Boko Haram guns, either. It cannot be. My husband is right beside me on the mattress.

He leaps out of bed, grabs his gun from beside his laptop, and changes his mind about wearing his boots. However, he remembers to pull on his mask before scurrying out of sight like a cockroach caught napping under an old carton.

I am not sure whether to wait for his return or if I should get up and leave the tent without his permission or instruction.

Through the tarpaulin, men's shadows dart to and fro like confused ghosts. I hear the bustling of running feet and the rustling of muttered exchanges. Then the muttering grows to a grumbling and the grumbling grows to a mighty rumbling. Soon, the entire camp is tumbling with footsteps and voices.

Boom! Boom! Boom!

The blasts appear much nearer to my ears than before. I stand up, climb into my skirt, pull on my niqab. But I cannot get up and leave the tent without his permission. I sit on the mattress and wait.

Boom! Boom! Boom!

It sounds like guns. Like bombs. Like an approaching army.

But every army in the world is afraid of Boko Haram. Fanne told us so. Even seasoned soldiers drop their weapons and flee at the sight of the rijale. No military would dare penetrate the Sambisa to attack.

My husband dashes back in. I am relieved to see him. I was afraid that he might forget that I was still here. Without looking at me, he grabs his laptop and forces his feet into his boots.

"Pack everything," he says. "We need to leave this place. Now."

At last, I can get up and leave.

I gather his clothes and bedding into a bundle.

"Go and load everything in the truck," he says. "Quick!"

I am unsure which of the dozens of trucks parked at the camp's edge he has in mind. But I obey and run outside. Suddenly, I halt, turned into a pillar of salt. The sight that meets my eyes is even more shocking than the raw terror in my husband's voice.

Great Boko Haram men, small Boko Haram men, lean Boko Haram men, brawny Boko Haram men, brown-skinned Boko Haram men, dark-skinned Boko Haram men, light-skinned Boko Haram men, veteran fighters and new recruits—all scampering about in panic, like bats disturbed from their cave. What could be alarming the rijale so?

Surely anything that makes a crocodile scamper in fear should be equally fearsome to a common lizard? I pick up my feet and run.

I am not the only woman rushing toward the trucks with an armful of domestic belongings. All around, children cry, or stand and stare.

Just as I dump my husband's property into the back of the nearest truck, its engine growls to life. A bunch of Boko Haram men clamber and scuffle aboard. They step on each other's feet. They stare into each other's fear-stricken eyes. They hold each other's hands and pray. These men are capable of feeling the same kind of terror they inflict on others. The same way they can also feel grief at a loved one's death.

Some Boko Haram men are more concerned for their lives, scrambling aboard every available truck and van and motorbike. Some do not want to leave behind their wives and the other women and girls they got as slaves. They drag them along into the trucks.

A hand grabs my arm. I jolt.

My husband.

"Get in the truck," he says.

Right there and then, I wonder why I never clawed out his eyeballs with my nails while he snored soundly. I wonder why I never smashed in his skull with his laptop. I tear my arm out of his grip and run.

"Salamatu! Salamatu!" His voice fades into the background. "You can never run away from me! Wherever you go, I will come and find you!"

More and more of us are tearing ourselves away from the Boko Haram men and running. Some of us head toward the deserted tarpaulin tents. Some head toward nearby trees and shrubs. With each sprint, I keep expecting to feel his grip around my arm or neck.

Fanne and some other wives are inside the trucks, happy to go along with their men. But when the vehicles are too full to take everyone, the men begin to push some of the women out of the truck.

And then the stones begin to rain.

The first one whizzes past my left ear. The second one strikes my shoulder.

"Ow!"

I stop running and crouch.

The air around me is crammed with screams. A child yelps and drops to the ground. A woman holds her baby to her stomach and wails, then doubles over to protect the child. A quick glance confirms what I already suspected. The rijale are pelting us with stones.

They would rather stone us to death than leave us behind alive.

By the time the *Boom! Boom! Boom!* is close enough to force the Boko Haram men into their trucks and away, many of us are lying with swollen eyes or bruised shoulders or broken heads squirting blood.

By the time the first armored tank with a green-white-green Nigerian flag draped in front appears, I am convinced that any hell outside must be better than life in this camp.

I forget about the aches on my arms and legs and fly toward the tank. Three girls have already flung themselves on the flag ahead of me.

. . . And I must not omit to say
That in Transylvania there's a tribe
Of alien people who ascribe
The outlandish ways and dress
On which their neighbors lay such stress,
To their fathers and mothers having risen
Out of some subterraneous prison
Into which they were trepanned
Long time ago in a mighty band . . .

—Robert Browning, "The Pied Piper of Hamelin"

ENGLISH WORDS

UNITED NATIONS.

International Committee of the Red Cross.

Believers' LoveWorld.

The first English words I have seen in a long time.

WHITE PEOPLE

Tall, small, lean, brawny.

Black hair, brown hair, white hair, golden hair. One with red hair, even!

Short sleeves, long sleeves, T-shirts, white coats. Colorful flat shoes with laces.

Tens and dozens, everywhere I look within the church premises converted into a camp for refugees.

Why are so many white people here, so close to Borno?

What are they doing in this place?

What business do they have with us?

What business do we have with them?

HIS VOICE

"Salamatu! Salamatu! You can never run away from me! Wherever you go, I will come and find you!"

His voice plays in my head when I lie down on the warm blanket that I have been given by the woman in a white T-shirt that has *UNICEF* written across the chest.

His voice plays in my head while I sit amid the hundreds of women and children on the floor of the refugee camp in Yola, all of us rescued by the Nigerian army. Some I recognize from my recent home in the Sambisa forest. Others I recognize from my previous home in the Sambisa forest.

The mere skin covering our bones and the plantations of insect bites make it clear which of us are from the forest and which are doctors and nurses and sundry good people who tell us through interpreters that they are here to help us.

"We will make sure you are in good health and that you are well taken care of," they say. "And we will also help you find your families."

I keep scanning the sea of faces for Zainab, craning my neck and waiting until the girl in a hijab raises her face or turns around in my direction. Maybe, just maybe.

Instead, I see Amira.

My heart stops, then starts banging like a drum.

But what do I have to fear from her?

Nothing. Not anymore.

I take in a deep breath.

The baby is sleeping peacefully in her lap. A white woman with *International Committee of the Red Cross* written across her back is stroking Amira's hand while she sheds tears into the edge of her hijab.

I wonder if she decided to stay back or if her husband pushed her out of the truck.

His voice plays in my head while one of the nurses in a blue uniform holds my hand and leads me behind the white sheet with which a section of the church hall has been cordoned off. The doctor's fingernails have no speck of dirt. He lowers his head gently and speaks in a soft voice while he pokes my chest and searches my throat and digs my belly and draws my blood.

The first white man I have touched in my life.

His voice plays in my head while a woman in a white T-shirt hands us chunks of fresh bread as thick as a child's head. When I am down to the last few delicious bites, I worry.

What if the next meal never comes?

STILL ALIVE

WHY DID I NOT take his life when I had the chance, blow his brains out when he was fast asleep or stick a knife into his throat?

How will I ever sleep easy knowing that he is out there somewhere, still alive, looking for me?

I STILL REMEMBER

Abraham,
    Elijah,
    Caleb,
    Isaac,
    Jacob . . .
    The names of all my brothers.

    Mathematics,
    English,
    Integrated science,
    Social studies,
    Religious knowledge . . .
    The subjects I learned in school.

    The acronym for:
    Brackets,
    Orders,
    Division,
    Multiplication,
    Addition,
    Subtraction . . .
    BODMAS: a useful reminder on the procedure for solving
mathematical equations.

Government of the people,
For the people,
And by the people . . .
The definition of democracy.

Our Father, who art in heaven,
Hallowed be thy Name,
Thy kingdom come,
Thy will be done,
On earth as it is in heaven.
Give us this day our daily bread.
And forgive us our trespasses,
As we forgive those
Who trespass against us.
And lead us not into temptation,
But deliver us from evil . . .
Our Lord's Prayer.

THE MAN IN THE MASK

COULD HE BE THE man handing out plastic bottles of water?

Could he be the man setting up tents with white plastic sheets?

Could he be the man placing the babies on a scale before replacing them in their mothers' arms?

Could he be the man driving the truck with a water tank?

Could he be the man arguing with the army officer, telling him that this camp is too full to take any more refugees, any more of the women and girls who disappeared?

Could he be the man asking each girl and woman her name, age, and village, and recording the information in a laptop?

I still do not know what my husband looks like in the daytime.

He could be any one of the men all over the place, pretending that, like them, he is here to help.

FREE MEDICAL TEST

PAPA WAS RIGHT. THE free health check people bring bad news.

Terrible, horrible news.

They tell me that I am pregnant.

BETTER LIFE

HOW WILL THE MOTHER of a child with bad blood lift her head high among normal human beings?

Life in the forest might have been better for me.

NEW DREAMS

I HOPE MY BABY will be a girl.

I do not want a boy who will grow up to be a rijale like his father, or a child who will look like him instead of like me.

TABLETS AND CAPSULES

THE TODDLERS ARE GIVEN a different combination with their meals.

The women and girls are given another combination with their meals.

The pregnant women and girls are given yet another combination. One gets stuck in my throat and I cough it out into my hand.

I am about to throw it back in my mouth when the nurse speaks softly.

"Go ahead and swallow it," she says. "It will be good for your baby."

I stare at the fat, oval, yellow capsule in my palm. I want to fling it in the sand and crush it with my toe.

But the nurse is watching.

I throw the capsule back inside my mouth and gulp.

Next time, I will hide it behind my molar until she moves on with her tray of tablets and capsules, on to the next girl who is pregnant with the child of a Boko Haram beast.

BUT

WHAT IF A DOCTOR's child does not bother going to university to learn? Will it automatically also become skilled in treating complicated diseases?

Why, then, is the case of Boko Haram children different?

How is it possible that they inherit their parents' beliefs?

THE PINK VAN

My EYES FOLLOW THE pink van as it moves into the camp premises. Hardly a head turns as the woman in the shiny braids parks her Keep a Girl in School van.

She parks it beside the International Committee of the Red Cross van.

Which is beside the UNICEF van.

Which is beside the Médecins Sans Frontières van.

Which is beside the Save the Children van.

Which is beside the Amnesty International van.

Which is beside the Murtala Muhammed Foundation van.

Which is beside the Human Rights Commission van.

Which is beside the National Emergency Management Agency van.

Which is beside the State Emergency Management Agency van.

Which is beside the Christian Association of Nigeria van.

Which is beside the European Union van.

Which is beside the BBC van.

Which is beside the CNN van.

Which is beside the Al Jazeera van.

Which is beside the Nigerian Television Authority van.

Which is beside the water truck.

Which is beside the Nigerian military truck.

My turquoise satchel that has "UNICEF" inscribed from one strap across to the other already contains two full packets of sanitary pads, which I will sadly not need for the next few months; nevertheless, I stretch out my hand and grab the pink packet that the woman passes to each girl.

I raise the packet to my nose and sniff.

I am overwhelmed by a strong desire to be seated at my desk in school, to be flipping through my textbooks or answering one of Malam Zwindila's many questions.

RESCUE

A MAN WALKS UP to me and squats by my side. I shudder. Could this be my husband, without his mask?

"I am from the Bring Back Our Girls group," he says in Hausa. "We have been campaigning to make sure that all the girls stolen by Boko Haram are returned to their families." He gestures toward his left. "This woman here is from the United States of America. She wants to ask you some questions."

That is when I notice the tall woman by his side.

Her nose is pointed. Her lips are thin. Her hair is black and shiny, so long and so straight, as if you could thread your needle and stitch a loose hem with each strand.

In her hand is a pen and notebook.

I wonder if I will remember how to hold a pen. I wonder what my handwriting looks like now.

"Is it okay for me to ask you some questions?" she asks.

I nod. I have forgotten how to say no.

She talks rapidly, shooting her words through her nose, so I am happy to have the man interpret, even though I still remember some of the English I learned in school.

"How old are you?"

"What is the name of your village?"

"When were you kidnapped?"

From time to time, she scribbles.

The questions become more and more difficult as she proceeds, experiences I am ashamed to share, especially not with a stranger. My fingers twist and twirl around each other in my lap, like tadpoles in a pond.

I stop answering.

"It's important that you tell her your story," the man says. "You have to tell her everything that happened. That is the only way the world can know, so that they can continue to look for the other stolen girls and rescue them from Boko Haram."

My story could help find Sarah?

And maybe Jacob as well?

"There were also boys taken," I say. "They didn't take only girls."

"Good. You have to tell her everything. Everything. That's the only way the world can know."

QUESTIONS AND ANSWERS

THE WOMAN FROM THE United States of America is back yet again with more questions for answers that will help the world find Sarah and Jacob.

I still cannot take my eyes away from her hair.

"You can touch my hair if you want," she says.

She smiles.

I smile.

AISHA

I WHIMPER.

I snivel.

I blubber.

I bawl.

At long last, I am shedding tears for my precious friend Aisha.

The woman from the United States of America does not know Aisha and neither does the man from Bring Back Our Girls. Still, the two of them cry along with me, and give me tissues to dry my eyes.

CHARLIE AND THE
CHOCOLATE FACTORY

I TAKE THE BOOK from her and stare at the curious artwork.

An old man in a hat, and a boy with golden hair waving a piece of paper.

Purple and yellow cover, brown pages, 192 in total, illustrations in black-and-white.

"I hope you like it," says the woman from the United States of America. "I got it specially for you."

A book specially for me?

"Willy Wonka's famous chocolate factory is opening at last!" I read silently from the back flap. "But only five lucky children will be allowed inside."

Amazing. Another world strange and new.

Suddenly, like an eagle trapped in a coop but whose heart remains in the sky, I am eager to break loose and fly high.

Whatever happens next, whatever lies ahead, I want to go back to school.

FOUND

"I WANT TO SEE the list of names," he says. "I was informed that some of our daughters are here, some girls from our village."

I recognize his voice as soon as I hear it.

I freeze.

The inflections, the emphasis on the first, second, and third words of his sentences, the firmness mixed with gentleness . . . everything is familiar.

I turn.

He leans his hands on the table, talking to the man sitting with the laptop.

I swing my head away, hiding in shame.

Too late. He has already seen me.

He screams my name and hops over five people's heads to get to me.

He grabs my neck and gathers me into his arms.

"Thank you, God! Your mother never stopped praying that God would bring you back home to her! She knew that you would come home one day!"

There are tears in Pastor Moses's eyes.

I cry.

To think that I will soon hear "Ya Ta" again.

AFTERWORD:
THE CHOSEN GENERATION

WE COULD CALL THEM "the Chosen Generation," borrowing from a popular Nigerian gospel song. They are girls that were supposed to be more fortunate than their mothers. They had better access to education. They would have a chance to make their dreams come true. Yet something changed along the way.

Since 2009, the terrorist group Boko Haram has been fighting an armed insurgency with the aim of creating an Islamic state in northern Nigeria. More than twenty thousand people have been killed and over two million displaced by the fighting, and, in a disturbing trend, thousands of women and girls have been abducted and raped.

One of these abductions received worldwide media coverage, at least for a while: on April 14, 2014, Boko Haram kidnapped 276 girls from their secondary school dormitory in Chibok, a small town in northeast Nigeria. In the middle of the night, they put the students on trucks and carried them away into the darkness of the Sambisa forest. Fifty-seven girls managed to escape by jumping off the trucks as they trundled into the night; 219 were taken away.

Yet to this day, few people around the world know any of these young women's names. They are just numbers. They are faceless.

Adaobi and I—a Nigerian and an Italian, a local woman and a foreigner—decided to document this tragedy in a way that nobody else had done: from the point of view of the girls and their families. We met in Abuja about one year after the Chibok kidnapping. I wanted to write a book for teenagers, and I had gotten in touch with the Bring Back Our Girls activists, who were campaigning for the girls' return. I didn't know Adaobi, but after reading an article of hers that appeared in the Italian newspaper *Corriere della Sera*—a moving letter to the kidnapped girls—I contacted her via email. She said she was also thinking about writing a book.

We decided to embark on this project together. I was thinking about nonfiction, while Adaobi wanted to write a novel because—as she pointed out—we didn't know how this story would end. I flew to Nigeria; I had arranged to meet some of the girls' families who had fled to Abuja, and we went to their houses together. We conducted interviews with the girls' parents—some in person and others over the phone. In 2016, we published another book in Italy, *Ragazze Rubate* (Mondadori), which is half fiction and half nonfiction; and I participated in a project led by Adaobi for the Murtala Muhammed Foundation, a Nigerian organization that wanted to collect every name and story of the Chibok girls.

There were challenges. It could be painful for the parents to talk; sometimes when I called them on the phone, I sensed that they had hoped it would be somebody bringing news rather than another journalist asking more questions. However, they often decided to talk to the media because it was their only way to keep the story alive. Some of the accounts contradicted one another, either because parents weren't completely honest or because they simply did not know much about their daughters' lives.

The biggest challenge for me was access to the most remote areas of Nigeria. When Adaobi managed to go to Chibok with a group of journalists, we decided that, because the situation was still volatile, I would endanger them because I am white and I would have attracted attention to the group. I had to stay behind. Despite the challenges, we followed developments closely every day for years, getting to know the parents and hoping for the girls' return.

We learned about their best friends and favorite songs. We could imagine their daily lives: helping their mothers and fathers in the house and on the farm. They taught their siblings and played with them. They lived in a part of Nigeria where losing a child to infection, fever, diarrhea, and other treatable maladies is a common experience for mothers—109 out of every 1,000 children die in northeast Nigeria, the highest infant mortality rate in the country.

They lived in Borno State, where women marry early, and the fact that they were going to school was impressive. More than half of the teenage girls in this part of the country have never studied at all, and only three out of ten will go to high school. After marriage, only a few continue to go, and that is only with the consent of their husbands.

We wanted these girls to be seen not just as numbers but as the curious, ambitious, and lovely daughters whom their families wanted to see again.

We wanted their parents' anguish to be understood. Their daughters were taken alive, but not knowing what had happened to them was, in some ways, worse than if they had died. Their parents couldn't mourn. They lived in limbo.

Rebecca Yishaku is one of the fifty-seven Chibok girls who escaped by jumping from the truck.

Rebecca was twenty-one, with a round face and lips like blooming flowers. When I interviewed her, she had returned to school, but had moved to Abuja, where she lived with an older sister. She liked to wear gold hoops in her ears and her hair gathered atop her head in a colorful scarf. Her widening hips announced her womanhood, but her voice remained like that of a child.

What struck me when I talked to her over the phone was the incredible guilt that she feels for leaving behind her best friend, Saraya Yanga. A year and a half after the kidnapping, Rebecca told me that she still saw Saraya and the other abducted girls in her nightmares. She pictured them deep in the forest, and they asked her how it was that she could have abandoned them.

Rebecca and Saraya had met in school three years earlier. They commissioned identical outfits with short pink and yellow skirts, orange tops, and shoes to match; they planned to wear them to the end-of-school celebration. They didn't want to get married after high school like many girls their age in the village. They wanted to continue their education. But first, they had to finish their secondary school exams, which would take place on April 14. Then they would be off to the next adventure: the university in Maiduguri.

Maiduguri, eighty miles away from Chibok, with its bustling, tree-lined streets, businesses, and bookstores, seemed like a big city to the girls from the village. It has a population of more than a million people and is home to one of the best universities in Nigeria. "Saraya wanted to study law, while I wanted to study economics because I like math," Rebecca told me.

Maiduguri was also the birthplace of Boko Haram.

Despite Nigeria being the largest oil producer in Africa, corrupt political elites monopolized the oil wealth while the vast majority of the citizens have seen little or no economic benefits, even in the oil-producing regions of the southern Niger Delta. Following numerous coups and countercoups, a fragile democracy emerged, but the country, with its 186 million inhabitants and more than 500 different ethnicities, remained roughly divided in two parts: the Muslim north and a predominantly Christian south with its Western-style education that had been spread by missionaries. A steep drop in agricultural production has damaged the mostly agrarian northern part of the country, with the resultant rural to urban migration.

The poverty, unemployment, and illiteracy in the north proved to be a breeding ground for extremism. Beginning around the year 2000, twelve northern Nigerian states, including Borno, adopted Sharia law: a collection of rules and principles based on an interpretation of Islam's sacred texts. Amputations and floggings, which had been banned, were reintroduced as punishments. Sharia coexisted, often contentiously, with civil law. Northern politicians had pushed for it; they used Sharia as a way to boost their popularity among the local population by promising a just society in the name of Islam. Corruption and abuse were still rampant, however, and people grew dissatisfied. Radical religious groups—including the one that would later become Boko Haram—initially allied themselves with those politicians, but later they turned against them.

In 2002, when Rebecca was just eight, a preacher named Muhammad Yusuf had founded a new mosque in Maiduguri after being cast out from other mosques for his extremist views. In his speeches, he laid blame on Western influence and education for the corruption of Nigeria's leaders. Northern Nigerians began to call his movement Boko Haram, which means "Western education is forbidden." His followers—some of whom were unemployed students and graduates—were mostly peaceful in spreading the group's ideas, despite some local skirmishes with policemen and rumors that they were stockpiling weapons. In 2007, following doctrinal differences between Yusuf and his former mentor, the latter was murdered inside his mosque.

When Rebecca was fifteen, in the summer of 2009, Boko Haram started an armed rebellion against the state to install a government based on Islamic law. The incident that sparked it was the killing of seventeen members by an anti-robbery task force after their alleged refusal to wear helmets while driving motorcycles at a funeral procession; this was largely seen as a pretext in a climate of building tension. Militants embarked on a violent and coordinated spree across northern Nigeria. The army crackdown left more than eight hundred people dead in five days, mostly members of the sect. Yusuf was arrested and executed, his mosque burned to the ground. But soon a new leader, Abubakar Shekau, was in place. He was more of an extremist than the founder. "Kill! Kill! Kill!" he shouted in one of his videos. "Now our religion is Kill! Kill! Kill!" He sent his followers to attack not only police and government facilities, but also both Christian and Muslim civilian targets.

On Sunday, April 13, 2014, Rebecca spent the day celebrating her sister Naomi's wedding in one of the dozens of churches that dotted the village of Chibok, springing up among the mud-brick houses along with several mosques. In the 1920s, missionaries from the Church of the Brethren, a denomination founded in Germany three hundred years ago, settled in this town in Borno State. Most of the sixty thousand village inhabitants were Christian, but there were also Muslim and mixed-religion families. Lawan Zanna, the secretary of the Parents of the Abducted Girls association, who is Muslim and whose daughter is one of the kidnapped girls, told me that people from the two faiths lived peacefully together, sometimes as part of the same family. For instance, he is Muslim but has Christian relatives. One of the kidnapped girls, Hauwa Musa, who lived in Chibok with her Muslim grandmother, chose to convert to Islam, even though her father was Christian.

Like Rebecca, several of the kidnapped Chibok girls had spent the previous Sunday celebrating family weddings; one even got married several days before she was abducted. April, together with December, is the month for weddings in Chibok. No farming is done, so people are freer to attend. The militants from Boko Haram had attacked wedding parties in other villages in Borno State before the Chibok kidnapping. One time they pretended to be among the guests and opened fire on the other revelers, Christian and Muslim alike, as they were delivering their gifts. Another time they massacred the faithful after a Muslim wedding. Fortunately, this had never happened in Chibok, but the northeast was in a state of emergency, and the government was underestimating the crisis gripping this part of the country.

Fear of Boko Haram existed in both communities, regardless of religion or ethnicity. Everyone knew that schools were a target too; the militants had burned fifty of them in Borno State, and another sixty had closed out of fear. In the neighboring state of Yobe, Boko Haram had locked fifty-nine male students in their dormitory and burned them alive. In Chibok, school had been suspended for a month but then had reopened. The Government Girls Secondary School in Chibok was the only one for miles that was open for end-of-year exams.

On Monday, April 14, hundreds of boys and girls from the town and the surrounding area passed through the gate of the Chibok school. The boys were day students, while the girls were boarders. After her English test, Rebecca returned to her dormitory to study for the next day's exams. Soon dusk began to rob the light of the day, leaving a pleasant coolness in exchange. With no electricity, the girls retired to their rooms, some of them using flashlights to read in the dark, and others drifting off to sleep.

It was a quarter to midnight when Rebecca woke with a start to the sound of shooting. Suddenly, she heard the rumble of motorbikes. A group of men entered the school. They were wearing military uniforms. One after the other, they filled the courtyard with the intense smell of their sweat. There were dozens, all of them armed with guns.

They forced the girls into the courtyard, just like a morning assembly. The two watchmen who were supposed to guard the entrance to the school weren't there. It's over, thought

Rebecca. But to her surprise, she remained calm. She felt like she was the only girl who had not shed a tear.

According to different survivors' accounts, the men asked where they could find the "brick-making machine" or the "engine block": it appears that their initial purpose was not to kidnap the girls but to steal machinery to use for house building or vehicles that they wrongly thought was kept in the school. In the pantry they only found sacks of rice, beans, pasta, and corn, which they loaded onto a truck. Then they began dousing the school with gasoline and setting fire to the classrooms and the abandoned teachers' quarters.

One of the men ordered the girls to wear their hijabs, but only a few took their veils out of their bag, put them on their heads, and wrapped them around their necks. The others remained seated in silence.

"You're Christian; you don't have a hijab, eh? Are you all Christian?"

The girls nodded.

"Does that mean we have to kill them?" asked one of the militants.

"Yes, we have to burn them too!" commanded another.

"No. Take all of them, Christian and Muslim. Let's go!" decided the captain. "Get up! Get up! And follow the road!"

The girls began to walk through the darkness, their only source of light the headlights from the truck and motorbikes. They were a human sea, at once silent, then trembling and crying. Whoever resisted or stopped was subject to a blow from a koboko. With Saraya beside her, Rebecca cast tears from her mind and looked for an opportunity to escape.

They walked and walked, for at least half an hour, and then they stopped under a tree. There were open pickups waiting, and the militants were loading some of the food onto them. Then they announced: "If you want to live, get on board. If you want to die, stay here!" Rebecca climbed up onto one of the trucks, Saraya at her side, and the others did the same. They were pressed together like in a cattle car, crouching among the sacks of rice and corn.

"We need to jump out," whispered Rebecca.

"I'm scared," Saraya cried.

All around the trucks buzzed the motorbikes, each one carrying three militants. If they tried to jump, they would be seen.

"God help us," prayed Rebecca.

But Saraya began to cry even harder. "You can't. I won't let you. You could get hurt. If you fall, you'll die."

"If I die, at least my family will have a body to cry over." Rebecca prayed a second and a third time. Then she squeezed her friend's hand and jumped over the side.

She landed on the ground and sprung to her feet. She dove under a tree and pressed her belly into the cold earth. After the next vehicle passed, she sought refuge under a large bush, and she waited for the last sound of the engines to die away and for the dust to settle. She waited, straining her ears for the sound of Saraya's voice. Then she plunged blindly into the maze of acacias, *dogonyaro*, and baobabs where one could get lost even during the day. She ran hour after hour, without stopping for anything: not her bloody feet, nor the branches that scratched her face, nor hunger, nor thirst. She pushed her legs forward. Her heart sank like a stone: Saraya had let go of her hand.

At the first light of dawn, she saw an unmistakable sign that she was on the right track. On the horizon she could see the smoke rising from her school as it burned. When she arrived at the nearby village of Bawa, the people surrounded her: "Our girl!"

They took her back to the school in Chibok. All that remained were the blackened walls and gutted roofs, the twisted frames of bunk beds and the books, binders, and uniforms that lay scattered across the ground. The families of many students had gathered there looking for their loved ones. Many of them were in shock and in tears. Her father was among them; he cried as he embraced her.

"Where are the others?" everyone asked.

"They aren't here anymore." Rebecca sighed. "My friends aren't here anymore."

More than two hundred fathers, uncles, and brothers gathered on motorbikes, determined to follow the tire tracks left by the militants. They had collected twelve thousand naira, about forty-three dollars, to offer as ransom. They were armed with old rifles, swords, and amulets.

They followed a trail of hair bands caught in trees, shreds of blue-checkered fabric, and discarded shoes.

They pressed forward into the Sambisa forest, zigzagging between the potholes. They arrived in a clearing where a few huts sat clustered. A group of women poked their heads out of the doorways.

"We're coming from Chibok; our girls have been kidnapped."

The women said they had seen the trucks. "But we can't go with you. The most that we can do is show you which way they went."

They came to a stream and pushed their bikes across the small bridge. The whole forest was plunged into absolute silence. No tweeting of birds, no rustle of lizards. A shepherd stepped out from the bush with his goats. "Sure, I saw your girls. Keep going this way and you'll find them."

After a while they arrived at a fork in the road. There was another old shepherd there. He seemed surprised to see them. "Yes, this is the way. They made them get out of the trucks and they took them on foot into the heart of Sambisa. But if you go in there like this, with those meager weapons and without the help of soldiers, you'll be killed together with your daughters. Turn around, wait for reinforcements. I've never seen anyone other than the men from Boko Haram go into this part of the forest and come back alive."

Evening fell. There were fifteen men left. They thought of their wives who would become widows, and their sons and daughters who would become orphans. They cried like children as they turned their bikes toward Chibok.

From deep in the forest came the echo of machine guns. The militants were training. Their daughters were so close.

After the Chibok kidnapping, a movement called Bring Back Our Girls was born out of rage and frustration against a government that had not taken the threat of Boko Haram seriously and was not doing enough to free the hostages.

The activists have met every day next to the Abuja Hilton, a few feet from the Fountain of Unity, and in other big cities, far away from Chibok, but they have helped draw attention to the forgotten plight in the northeast of their country.

In May 2014, more than four million people used the hashtag #BringBackOurGirls—including Malala Yousafzai, the youngest Nobel Peace Prize winner, and Michelle Obama—to express their solidarity with the relatives of the kidnapped students. Malala went to Nigeria that summer, met with Rebecca Yishaku and four other escapees, and criticized the government's weak efforts to free their kidnapped friends. World leaders from the United States to China promised to help find the girls. In particular, the US and UK governments conducted surveillance operations. Nigerian president Goodluck Jonathan welcomed financial and logistical aid and assistance by the US, the UK, and France. For its part, the US government was concerned about sending military help and about stronger cooperation with the Nigerian army, which had been accused of human rights violations, including the killing of innocent civilians in sweeps for Boko Haram.

The Nigerian government banned the Bring Back Our Girls protests at one point, explaining that there was a risk of their gatherings being targeted by suicide bombers. Supporters of the government pelted the activists with rocks and bottles and threw and scattered their chairs at the sit-ins. In the 2015 presidential election, Goodluck Jonathan was defeated by Muhammadu Buhari, a former Nigerian army major general. His loss was due in part to his handling of the Chibok crisis and his underestimation of the Boko Haram threat; in 2014 the group managed to declare a caliphate in the northeastern states under its control. President Buhari has confronted Boko Haram more seriously, working as part of a military coalition with Cameroon, Chad, Benin, and Niger, which share a border with Nigeria and are also heavily affected by the militants. After Buhari's election, military relations with America have warmed.

Nothing has stopped the activists. For the first anniversary of the kidnapping on April 14, 2015, they marched through Abuja with red tape covering their mouths. I went to one of the protests, in June 2015, where a woman in a red hijab standing in front of a sign with the slogan "Bring Back Our Girls" was shouting with her fist in the air:

"What do we demand?"

"To bring our girls back home: Now! Alive!" the other activists in red shirts responded, seated on plastic chairs in the humid afternoon.

"What are we asking for?"

"The truth! Nothing but the truth!"

"When will we stop?"

"Only when our girls come home alive!"

"What are we fighting for?"

"For the soul of Nigeria!"

"The struggle for the Chibok girls is the struggle for the soul of Nigeria!"

After more than two years, however, many relatives had stopped going to the meetings. Some of them died from what they call high blood pressure, which might be another name for a broken heart. Many families fled Chibok after repeated attacks by Boko Haram. Some of them found refuge in the periphery of Abuja, but they didn't have the money to make the daily trip to the Fountain of Unity.

One of the most vocal mothers is Esther Yakubu. Her daughter Dorcas was seized two months before her sixteenth birthday.

When I first called, her husband Yakubu Kabu answered the phone; he seemed unsure whether to meet with me. That day, two French television journalists had visited the family; Esther cried on camera remembering her daughter Dorcas, and she felt sick. In the last two years Esther had asked for help from the government, had joined the protests, and had even gone on TV to plead her case. She had heard it all: false claims and false reports, including ones that maintained that her child had been released or that she hadn't really been kidnapped in the first place, that it was all a political plot. At one point, Esther refused to eat. She stopped sleeping. She was like a candle burning down to its base. Her husband felt that Esther had endured enough and didn't want her to meet any more reporters, but in the end the couple changed their mind; talking about Dorcas was painful, but they needed to fight for her.

They welcomed Adaobi and me into a small room on the outskirts of Abuja, where they had moved to escape the renewed attacks by Boko Haram in Chibok. Kabu had worked as a driver, Esther as a municipal employee, but now they were both unemployed. Yet they still made sure they would send their other four children to school.

It was a very hot summer day with a single fan blowing in the corner. Dorcas's parents and their four younger children—Happy, Marvelous, Messi, and Mercy—sat on a mattress on the floor. The room was bare, except for framed pictures of Esther and Kabu. She was wearing her cap and gown; her picture was taken after she graduated from the polytechnic in Maiduguri. Esther had promised her daughter that if she got good grades, she would allow her to continue her education as well, but had also planned for her to take a sewing course, because it would be useful in case she could not find work. In fact, Esther had already bought her a sewing machine. Dorcas didn't know; it was going to be a surprise graduation gift.

Although they lived in Chibok, Dorcas transferred to the local secondary school only a few months before the kidnapping. She was initially studying in Maiduguri, but something had happened that had really upset her: Boko Haram had kidnapped two boys off the street. They were swallowed up by the Sambisa forest, probably to be turned into militants. Dorcas didn't know the boys, said her mother, but the same thing could happen to anyone. Along the road, frightened boys would ride their bikes carrying bows and arrows to defend themselves, but they would be useless against the AK-47s of Boko Haram. Eventually the road to Maiduguri, littered with the carcasses of dead cars, was closed. It would take two days to get to the city now, passing through the tiny villages in the surrounding area. Vigilantes would stop every car, brandishing machetes and ordering them to turn on their windshield wipers; they were often disconnected if there were weapons hidden under the hood.

Chibok seemed safer. However, there had been some alarms. Esther Yakubu and other parents consider the school authorities responsible for the kidnapping, although they can't say whether it was a plot or negligence. All the teachers sleeping on campus that night had fled when Boko Haram attacked, abandoning the students.

The last time Dorcas came home was three weeks before April 14. Her last words to her mother were: "I'm praying that the last exam goes well!" Dorcas slept at the dorms so that she could concentrate on her studies, but also because the vice principal had forbidden the girls from leaving the school grounds, even with a five-day break between one test and the next. While some girls risked punishment—jumping over the low wall that surrounded the campus and running home—Dorcas had followed the rules and stayed at school all weekend.

Esther told us that one evening, several weeks before the kidnapping, some of the secondary school's girls had shouted: "Boko Haram! Boko Haram!" They climbed the gate and ran toward the village. They thought they had seen men approaching the school. Her youngest sister, Happy, was among the girls who ran home, while Dorcas had gone to fetch water from the well and barely noticed. After that episode, the principal gathered the students and assured them that they had only mistaken some girls in pants for the militants. Both the principal and a senior army officer from the local garrison gave them an order: "If you really do see Boko Haram, don't shout. Don't run. Stay inside and gather together." Because of this order, when the militants went to the school, the girls did not try to escape and were easily captured by Boko Haram. "If they had told them: 'Do not scream, but try to escape,' they would have run," Esther said.

Some survivors have related another detail to journalists: A few days before the kidnapping, the girls saw the vice principal pick up a piece of paper from the ground. It said, "BOKO HARAM IS COMING." They wondered whether the exams would be postponed and the school closed again, but the principal had reassured them that there was only one thing coming for them: the exams.

Esther showed us a photo of Dorcas that was taken in the sunny courtyard of her school on April 13, the day before she was kidnapped. She had given it to a *massa* vendor who lived near her home so that she would deliver it to her parents. They planned to use it in an almanac, to give as a gift to friends and relatives waiting to celebrate the graduation of their firstborn daughter. It turned out to be the last contact they had with Dorcas.

Dorcas and her mother, Esther, had the same almond-shaped eyes and decisive character. Esther remembers an obedient girl who woke up at dawn, collected water at the river, prepared supper, and bathed her four younger siblings, all while singing gospel songs. Her favorite was "I Know Who I Am," which is popular on the radio as well as in churches in Nigeria.

> *We are a chosen generation*
> *Called forth to show His excellence*
> *All I require for life, God has given me*
> *And I know who I am.*

Happy still sings "We Are a Chosen Generation" alone. It's all that is left of her sister. When she talked about her she smiled, but the smile would suddenly fade away.

Dorcas shared her secrets with two people. The first was her grandma, Hauwa, who suffered for Dorcas's loss as if her own child had been taken from her womb, said Esther. Her second confidante was Saraya Stover, her best friend. Dorcas's sister Happy explained that Dorcas and Saraya were inseparable. "They ate from the same plate, they sang the same songs." One of them wanted to be a teacher, the other a doctor. They were kidnapped together.

About one year after our meeting, in the summer of 2016, Esther's belief that her daughter was still alive was vindicated. On August 14, Dorcas appeared for the first time in a Boko Haram video: she was the spokesperson for dozens of veiled girls who were prisoners just like her. She introduced herself as Maida, her middle name. "We are not happy here. I plead with our parents to meet with the government in order to release the Boko Haram men kept as prisoners, so that we can also be released." Her face was visible but Esther and Kabu also clearly recognized her voice. It was the first proof that she was alive.

The Church of the Brethren, known as EYN—the Ekklesiyar Yan'uwa of Nigeria—is the most popular church in Chibok. Before the kidnapping and the displacement of many residents, Sundays would see seven hundred people arrive for the English service at seven a.m. and more than one thousand for the Hausa service at a quarter to ten.

Reverend Enoch Mark had moved to Chibok with his family about a year before to lead the congregation. His daughter Monica Enoch was also abducted on April 14. The reverend told me that she might be dead. One night she appeared to him in a dream wearing a long white dress, standing in the center of an open field, beneath an iron staircase suspended in the air. "Monica slowly climbed, step by step toward heaven," he said. Later on, however, Adaobi learned from the survivors that Monica might still be alive and could be one of the first girls who decided to marry a Boko Haram fighter, thinking that it would make it easier to escape.

Initially, Reverend Mark became a spokesperson for the parents of the abducted Chibok schoolgirls, but he told me that he was sidelined and threatened because of his fierce criticism of the government and of Boko Haram. He moved to the town of Mubi until Boko Haram attacked it, and then to Minna, where the family scraped by selling firewood.

The reverend could not remember his first daughter's birthday. He thinks that it was sometime in June 1993. He said that Monica's life revolved around God and that she would wake up at four a.m. humming her favorite hymn: "In the morning, early in the morning, I will rise and praise the Lord." He didn't tell me, however, that before the kidnapping Monica had married a soldier and had a child. She left him after her family discovered that the soldier had another wife and didn't tell the reverend and his daughter, who only discovered it later.

On that Monday in April, at five o'clock in the afternoon, Monica led the prayer in the Ghana Room at Chibok's secondary school. The Ghana Room was where the girls would meet, crouching on the floor, reading the Bible, praising the Creator, and, one after the other, adding a personal request, such as for Him to intercede on their behalf in the coming exams.

The reverend said he lost another daughter on April 14, since he had also adopted Monica's best friend, Sarah Samuel. A few months before the kidnapping, Sarah and her family had escaped from the nearby village of Banki, on the border with Cameroon, which had been attacked by Boko Haram. Adaobi and I interviewed her parents, Samuel and Rebecca Yaga, in the village of Kobi Makaranta in Abuja, where they had fled.

Sarah's father left his daughter behind in Chibok so that she could finish her exams. According to Reverend Enoch, instead of staying with her uncle, Sarah moved to his house and he took her in as one of his own.

On April 14, in the middle of the night, the phone rang in the reverend's house. It was a friend from the neighboring village. "A convoy of pickups and four-by-fours. They're overflowing. Boko Haram is coming."

Reverend Enoch Mark tried not to panic. He thought about the small platoon of fifteen soldiers stationed in Chibok and tried to call their post. During the sixth try, an explosion blew out the windows of his house. Then he ran with his wife and children into the forest. They found themselves together with other fleeing families, and the soldiers he'd been trying to call.

It was then that they heard the screams. Keen. Desperate. They came from the school. It was his daughters.

It went on for three minutes, but it felt like hours. Then a silence fell that chilled their blood even more than the screams.

At the first light of morning, the reverend went to search for Monica and Sarah in the forest.

"Your daughter Monica jumped out. She's hurt, and can't walk," somebody told him. But he didn't find them. He did find two other girls who had managed to escape, choked with dust and horror, and he took them home.

In the months and years after the kidnapping, the parents heard many things about the fate of their daughters. Rumors in the village said that they were taken by boat across Lake Chad, or over the hills of Gwoza, and that they were still among the caverns and valleys on the border with Cameroon. They said that the girls from Chibok were forced to convert, which in certain cases turned out to be true: according to a secret diary written by some of the survivors, on one occasion they were threatened to be burned with gasoline if they did not; at another time, they were told that they would be allowed to go home to their families only if they all converted. There were also many false rumors: that they were sold as slaves for two thousand naira apiece, or about seven dollars; and that they were learning to fight and kill, trained to cut prisoners' throats, or used as teachers to instruct the newcomers about the Quran (and whip them if they made mistakes).

The Nigerian government said that it had negotiated with Boko Haram, but the talks failed several times.

Meanwhile, the Chibok parents did not know what to believe, so they tried to verify the news themselves. At one point, in March 2016, a twelve-year-old suicide bomber was arrested in Cameroon before she could detonate the explosives strapped to her body. She claimed that she was from Chibok. Dorcas Yakubu's mother, Esther, stayed up late, waiting for a phone call. She thought that they would call her to let her know that the girl was her daughter; she even started planning the food she would cook to welcome her home. Yana Galang, mother of seventeen-year-old Rifkatu, another kidnapped Chibok student, was supposed to travel to Cameroon to verify the identity of the girl.

Yana has had a difficult life. Her husband left her for another wife in Maiduguri, and she has seven more children to feed working in the fields, but her determination is boundless. Just after the abduction, she was photographed sitting on the steps of her home, next to an open suitcase where she kept Rifkatu's few remaining dresses—orange and blue, white and pink—like a captured rainbow. She kept them there so that Rifkatu could find her things intact when she returned. Yana talked about her daughter as a fragile girl who was often sick but always in a good mood.

Rifkatu worked too much: in addition to studying and helping with the house chores, she braided hair for half the village because she wanted to help her mother financially, and when she saw Yana frown and worry, she would do anything to make her smile. After secondary school, Rifkatu could not continue her studies because she didn't have the money to go to university. She had to get married and move to Lagos.

During one of our most recent phone calls, Yana told me

that she was tired of talking about Rifkatu. She didn't want to speak of a past that, despite its hardships, she missed greatly. In the end, Yana and another member of the Chibok parents association who were supposed to go to Cameroon to identify the detained girl did not go. Instead they were just shown photographs, from which they concluded that the suspected suicide bomber wasn't a Chibok girl.

Boko Haram is infamous for using girls as young as seven as suicide bombers. From June 2014 to January 2016, according to the *Long War Journal*, an American nonprofit news website that reports on the war on terror, 105 women were used in suicide attacks in Nigeria. However, many people consider it unlikely that the Chibok captives were ever used as suicide bombers. It seems that, because of their notoriety, they were considered precious as bargaining chips or propaganda tools. To the world they have become a symbol of the violence committed by the militants, but Boko Haram—who followed the news closely— has turned them into a megaphone to advertise its ideology and demonstrate its strength. The paradox is that international attention might have made them more difficult to save.

The Chibok girls were reportedly "not forced" to wed the militants, but marriage was offered to them as a "choice"— although it did not happen without pressure. Those who refused were beaten and forced to serve as slaves to the militants' wives, who in turn became brutal with their former friends. According to survivors, some of the girls were also taken as concubines.

Among those who married is said to be the daughter of Lawan Zanna, the current secretary of the Parents of the Abducted Girls association. He imagined something different for Aisha. Asked whether he wanted her to get married at eighteen, he told me: "No, no, no." He hadn't even allowed her to have a cell phone because he was afraid it would distract her from her studies.

On Monday, April 14, Aisha asked him: "What gift will you give me at the end of the year?"

"If you get good grades, then I will send you to university," he replied. He hoped that his daughter would choose to study medicine. Of course, after she graduated he would also get her a phone.

One of Aisha's best friends, Hajara Isa, who could recite the Quran with the voice of an angel, had escaped from an arranged marriage three years before, at the age of fifteen. It was Hajara's aunt from Chibok who convinced the mother to wait three years to let the girl attend high school and "make something of herself in society."

In a souvenir photo she took at school, Hajara appeared with a golden-yellow head scarf over her luxurious black hair, and a dress in the same color. Her eyes were traced with black kohl, and her lips tinged with a touch of red. She looked very different in the first video released by Boko Haram, where all the girls were wearing hijabs of gray or black, covering them from head to toe. They were sitting with the palms of their hands turned skyward or their arms stretched atop their knees.

They had a lost look, and their voices mechanically recited verses from the Quran.

Hajara was the third to speak: "I am a Muslim from birth and my parents are Muslim as well. Contrary to what others have said, this group has treated us with love and care. I hope that other women will join us."

She seemed calm. It was impossible to tell what was going through her mind.

Her aunt said that she was supposed to participate in a prestigious Quran recitation contest in the state of Zamfara, but destiny brought her to recite her holy book for a group of killers.

Following Nigerian armed forces' operations, about three thousand women and girls have been rescued or managed to escape. None of them was from Chibok—until May 2016.

In June 2015, I went to Yola, a town in Adamawa State, where four hundred thousand displaced people (more than the population of the town) lived in forty-one informal refugee camps and a handful of government camps; 677 women had just been rescued and taken there, and the majority were pregnant. Everybody had a story about how the jihadists massacred the men and forced the women to have children by Boko Haram militants.

Religious leaders intervened to invite their families to welcome the women back, but their reintegration is difficult in both Christian and Muslim communities—especially in a society where there is a strong culture of honor based on a woman's body and her virginity.

At an informal camp in front of the Saint Theresa church, I met a ten-year-old girl, Semo. "I saw them enter the houses and kill the men, cutting their throats, shooting or burning them alive," she told me staring at the ground. "In the Sambisa forest, we lived in tin shacks. They taught us the Quran. They fed us two or three times a day: rice, maize, or yams. At night, they took some of the older girls; they brought them back in the morning. I cried and they asked me why, but I didn't answer. I was thinking of my parents."

In the refugee camp, Semo was living with displaced people from her hometown who protected her, but they told me that pregnant women would not be welcome. "It is better if they get an abortion."

Some people believe that Boko Haram's children will inherit their fathers' ideology and they will be a danger for the community. Even before any Chibok girl was freed, there were rumors about one of them coming back home at night and killing her sister in her sleep; another story said that a Chibok girl had killed her entire family.

Finally, in May 2016, more than two years after being kidnapped, the first Chibok girl was found wandering on the outskirts of the Sambisa forest by a group of soldiers and civilian vigilantes. Her name is Amina Ali. She was clutching a four-month-old baby and was in the company of a suspected Boko Haram militant, Mohammed, who claimed to be her husband.

Her rescue sparked new attention in the international media. The twenty-one-year-old and her daughter met with President Buhari, who held the child, Safiya, in front of the cameras. Mohammed was arrested.

Afterward, Amina did not return home. She was kept in a secret location in the capital, Abuja, for what the Nigerian government called a "restoration process."

Her mother, Binta Ali, was allowed to spend two months with her, but then she returned to Chibok. She is a widow who lost eleven of her thirteen children to different illnesses; Amina and her older brother, Noah, are her only family. According to the village doctor, she tried to commit suicide after Amina was seized. When she saw her daughter again for the first time, in May 2016, Binta Ali shouted her name: "Amina, Amina!" Then she hugged her and didn't let go, making Amina lose her balance. "Please, Mum, take it easy, relax," she said. "I never thought I would ever see you again, wipe your tears. God has made it possible for us to see each other again."

In August 2016, Amina gave Adaobi an interview. "I just want to go home," she said, speaking softly. "I am not scared of Boko Haram—they are not my God."

Before the abduction she had planned to go to university. After escaping the forest, she thought that she would get a sewing machine so that she could earn something making clothes. Eventually, she decided to resume her studies. Amina missed the father of her four-month-old baby girl, whom she married a year earlier. She said that they weren't rescued, they had chosen to escape together: "I want him to know that I am still thinking about him. Just because we got separated, that does not mean that I don't think about him."

She spoke about her experience of hunger in the forest, where the young women resorted to eating raw maize to survive. She said that some had died, suffered broken legs, or gone deaf due to explosions and air strikes by the Nigerian military. In August 2016, the terrorist group released another video showing the dead bodies of a dozen captives: a masked man said that they were killed in a government air strike. Amina confirmed that some of her classmates died in a bombing, but it had happened over a year before. She expressed confidence that the other girls could be freed. "In the same way God rescued me, he will also rescue them."

Two months later, in October 2016, her words were partially fulfilled. The first twenty-one Chibok girls were released. Their families drove to the capital through military checkpoints and braved terrorist attacks. Finally, they embraced their emaciated daughters, amid singing and dancing. In May 2017, eighty-two more girls were freed. In both cases they were reportedly exchanged for Boko Haram commanders and an undisclosed ransom running millions of dollars, following negotiations between the Nigerian government and the militants. The deal was brokered by the Swiss government and the International Red Cross and mediated by a lawyer from Maiduguri, Zannah Mustapha. An army raid into the forest liberated another girl, and yet another was found thanks to interrogation of suspects.

In 2007, Mustapha founded the Future Prowess Islamic Foundation school, offering free education, meals, and health care to both children born to Boko Haram fighters and those orphaned by the group's insurgency. He refused to close it, despite Boko Haram's attacks in the region, as he feared that the war was creating a generation of children with no education. With the help of the International Committee of the Red Cross, he also provided humanitarian assistance to the widows of Boko Haram militants, at a time when they were being arrested and their houses demolished by the government. Therefore, the insurgents respected him and the ICRC.

Mustapha denied that "any of the 103 girls were touched by anybody. None of them were abused." When I asked him how he knew, he replied: "I asked if they were abused, and they said no. One said that she had been married for three months before the abduction and she gave birth to a baby from before."

At the time, the rescued girls identified dozens of their classmates who had married fighters, and twelve who had died during Nigerian air force strikes, in childbirth, or from unknown illnesses. They also recognized some of the faces of the Boko Haram fighters on the government's most-wanted list.

The negotiations were complicated by the fact that Boko Haram has split. Initially faithful to Al Qaeda, in 2014 the group declared allegiance to ISIS. In August 2016 a faction, endorsed by ISIS, left Boko Haram leader Abubakar Shekau's group. Abu Musab Al Barnawi, the son of Boko Haram founder Muhammad Yusuf, is the faction's leader—or rather, the "governor" of the Islamic State's West Africa Province, as they like to call it. He disagrees with Shekau's attacks against Muslims based on the idea that those who choose not to engage in jihad are apostates who should be killed. But he promised more violence against Christians and their churches. Some experts believed that the girls still in captivity are held by Shekau's faction, which was said to be poorly armed and increasingly surrounded in the Sambisa forest. There is also a possibility that the two groups will fight each other, thus helping the government.

On May 12, 2017, Boko Haram published another video in which Dorcas Yakubu—now called Maida—appeared. This time, only her eyes were visible through the slit in her niqab. She didn't call herself a "prisoner" but a "bride," and she said that everyone should convert to Islam. "I don't want to go back to Chibok, I don't want to live in a town of unbelievers," she said.

According to negotiator Zannah Mustapha, Dorcas and a few others have refused to go home. It's difficult to understand why. Do they feel fear or shame? Do they really identify with their kidnappers? Are they unwilling to leave behind the lives they have built while in captivity? After all, three years is a long time. Clinical psychologist Dr. Fatima Akilu, head of Nigeria's deradicalization program, says that being a jihadi wife has its advantages over the "normal" life in a patriarchal society: they have power, slaves who clean and cook for them, and even the respect of men. When they are freed, kidnapped women face challenges reintegrating into a society that stigmatizes them.

The Chibok girls who have returned since 2016 discovered that they are not completely free. Initially they were not allowed to go back to their homes; they had to live in government buildings where they received medical and psychological help. There were fears that some might have been radicalized—that they identified with Boko Haram and could be a threat to other civilians. The government was also worried that the girls could be in danger if they returned home, that they could be kidnapped again. In September 2017, the 103 girls began a government-sponsored special catch-up course at the American University of Nigeria in Yola, but during their studies they were not allowed to leave the premises of the school.

After completing the course, the girls hoped that they would finally be permitted to go home.

Dorcas Yakubu's parents refuse to accept that their daughter might not want to come back. They think that maybe some of the girls are being forced to stay by their Boko Haram husbands and are just pretending, waiting to find a chance to escape. They ignore schoolmates who say that Dorcas was so radicalized that they feared her.

The sewing machine, her secret graduation gift, sits gathering dust in a forgotten corner in Chibok.

There are still more than one hundred Chibok girls in captivity along with many other women from other Nigerian towns. In addition, many of those who were freed have not been able to return to a normal life, because of stigmatization by the community and/or because of their own radicalization. What happened in Sambisa changed them forever. The Chibok girls are the most famous part of a lesser-known story. Even if all of them come home, the insurgency will still be there. Bringing peace to northeastern Nigeria is a process that will take a long time.

—Viviana Mazza

ACKNOWLEDGMENTS

Thank you to the dozens of Boko Haram victims who trusted us with their stories, in tremendous and shocking detail. We pray that they receive all the help they need to continue with their education and with the rest of their lives.